KING

OF

Durabia

Book 1 of the Knights of the Castle Series

Naleighna Kai

Macro Publishing Group
Chicago, Illinois

This is a work of fiction. Names, characters, places, and incidents are products of the author's imagination or are used fictitiously and are not to be construed as real. Any resemblance to actual events, locales, organizations, or persons, living or dead, is entirely coincidental.

King of Durabia by Naleighna Kai Copyright ©2020
ISBN: [Ebook] 9781952871009
ISBN: [Trade Paperback] 978-1-952871-08-5

Macro Publishing Group
1507 E. 53rd Street, #858
Chicago, IL 60615

Cover Designed by: J.L Woodson: www.woodsoncreativestudio.com
Cover Model: Vikkas Bhardwaj of www.vikkaszone.com
Interior Designed by: Lissa Woodson: www.naleighnakai.com
Editors: J. L. Campbell jlcampbellwrites@gmail.com
Janice M. Allen janiceallen7519@gmail.com
Betas: Debra J. Mitchell, Ellen Kiley Goeckler, Brynn Weimer

KNIGHT

OF

Durabia

Book 1 of the Knights of the Castle Series

Naleighna Kai

♦ DEDICATION ♦

Jean Woodson,
Eric Harold Spears,
LaKecia Janise Woodson,
Mildred E. Williams,
Anthony Johnson,
L. A. Banks,
Octavia Butler,
Tanishia Pearson Jones,
Emmanuel McDavid, and
Priscilla Jackson.

♦ ACKNOWLEDGEMENTS ♦

Special thanks goes out to: The Creator from whom all Blessings and opportunities flow, Sesvalah, my son, J. L. Woodson (for the awesome cover designs for the Knights of the Castle and the Kings of the Castle series), Janice M. Allen, Debra J. Mitchell, Royce Slade Morton, Bunny Ervin, J. L. Campbell, Kelly Peterson, Janine A. Ingram, Ehryck F. Gilmore, LaVerne Thompson, Kassanna Dwight, Vikkas Bhardwaj (our amazing cover model), Frankie Payne, Ella Houston, Betty Clawson, Amanda McCoy, Ellen Kiley Goeckler, Brynn Weimer, Theresa V. Wilson, Stephanie Fazekus-Hardy, Stephanie M. Freeman, Shae Cross, J. D. Mason, Unique Hiram, Siera London, Elizabeth Means, April Bubb, King Brooks,

the Kings of the Castle Ambassadors, Members of Naleighna Kai's Literary Cafe, the members of NK Tribe Called Success, the members of NAMAKIR Tribe, NAMISTE Tribe and to you, my dear readers . . . thank you all for your support.

Naleighna Kai

Chapter 1

"You risked your life for my grandson," Sheikh Aayan said, his voice echoing through the ornate throne room. "Ask for anything and I will see what can be done."

Ellena scanned the expectant faces of the throngs of people who had gathered for this unexpected audience with the ruler of Durabia. Most of their tunics and dishdashas differed from her casual attire of a simple white blouse and black slacks. "Thank you, but that isn't necessary. I did what anyone would do."

"Evidently, not everyone," he said, and his angry glare focused on the bodyguard, caregivers, and everyone who had stood by when Javed, the little royal, had swept past Ellena and landed on the moving conveyor belt.

All of them had frozen in place the moment Javed brushed against the rubber bounding strip and was sucked into the void. The video of Ellena dropping her tote bag, diving in after him, and cradling him in her arms as they were both tossed through the maze of steel and vinyl, all while being battered by suitcases and duffel bags alike, went viral.

Ellena had closed her eyes, bracing under each blow. Javed's laughter was a stark contrast to her pain. The cameras caught everything, including the tail end of the journey when Ellena tumbled out of the final drop onto another belt and finally into the metal cart that would carry the luggage onto the plane. Security finally found their legs and scrambled to make it to Ellena and the little boy before they sustained further injuries. Well, before she did. Her fleshy body was all the protection that Javed needed.

Javed Khan, a great grandson of the Royal Family, was completely unharmed. Ellena, on the day of arrival for a class reunion vacation, had to be rushed to the hospital. They kept her overnight. She sustained a few cuts and bruises that matched the dent in her ego when the entire world saw her tossed head over ass multiple times. And when the adrenaline wore off and the fear kicked in, the little royal refused to let her go. He even had to travel in the emergency transport with her because none of the guards or caregivers managed to force him to release his hold on Ellena.

Now she stood in a palace situated in the heart of a metropolis in the Middle East with a décor that was unrivaled by anything she'd ever seen. Gold—everything was layered with it—the walls, doors, accented by purples and reds that added a sultry warmth to all of the opulence of the furniture, paintings, and draperies covering massive windows.

"Well, to be honest, I haven't wanted much," she said with a nervous laugh. "And the only thing I don't have is a husband. But I'd love to have a place here in Durabia, where I can come and go as I please. If that is at all possible."

"Done," the Sheikh said, beckoning to the man who had visited the hospital twice to see about her condition. "Kamran, come."

"Wait. What?" She laughed and rested a hand on her ample bosom. "An apartment, really?"

"Your new husband," he answered with a grand gesture that would have made Vanna White proud. "This is my oldest son."

The man was drop-dead gorgeous. Olive complexion, dark hair, goatee neatly trimmed to perfection, and piercing brown eyes that missed nothing. He was more suited to a fashion runway than a palace. Truthfully, she wasn't sure if it was the tunics, neat beards, head coverings or what. Durabia seemed to have no shortage of handsome men. But the Sheikh's son was a masterpiece, exuding the kind of confidence that came with a man who was certain of his place in the world. His gaze swept across her face with a complexion slightly darker than his olive tone, then quickly covered the distance over her curves, then his lips lifted in a warm, appreciative smile that practically lit up his dark brown eyes and sent heat straight to places that had been dormant since the Queen of Sheba caused King Solomon to lose his entire mind.

Ellena shook her head, clearing her mind of all manner of wickedness that came after that wonderful assessment. "I think you misunderstood. I was joking about the husband part. The apartment, time share or whatever you call them here, that's all I really want."

"You will have both," the Sheikh commanded with a nod of finality no one would dare to question. "A husband and a place here. My son needs a wife and you mentioned you do not have a husband. Problem solved."

"But doesn't he have to give you heirs or something?" She instinctively brought her hands near her belly. "My eggs are old enough to be married and have children of their own by now."

First, a roar of laughter went up from him. A few moments later, it was mirrored by everyone standing around her. Yes, that line was funny, but the one thing she understood was the unfairness of the situation. At least for Kamran. And that was no laughing matter.

The Sheikh waved away that thought. "That will not be a concern. He is unable to give you or any woman children. And a woman of African descent will never sit on the Durabian throne. We are safe on that score."

A shadow of sadness flickered in Kamran's eyes and his skin flushed a shade darker. Ellena tried to read a deeper meaning into his father's words. She still came up with *unfair*. "So, you just throw him to a random woman because he can't give you an heir? He is *still* a man. He *still* has value," she insisted. "A brain, intelligence, and a purpose." She inhaled, trying to tamp down on her anger. "The apartment is fine, Sheikh. Thank you, but I will not be foisted on a man who has no say in the matter. That's downright cruel."

A gasp came from the core of people around them before silence descended in the room. Even Kamran flinched.

The Sheikh's face darkened with anger as he slowly came to his feet. "Are you refusing—"

"Give me nine days—"

All eyes focused on the handsome man, who left his father's side and moseyed toward her like some type of Arabian cowboy. All swagger, no gun necessary.

"Give me nine days," he repeated and moved across the expensive Persian carpet until he stood in front of her, towering over her near six-foot height by three inches of his own. "Nine days for me to show you Durabia, to answer any questions you may have. To let you explore the place, the people, the culture. Then you decide."

Ellena found it hard to catch her breath. The man was so virile she felt warm all the way to her follicles. "Nine days? I have to go home. I have a job back there. I used all of my vacation and two of my sick days for this trip."

"Your job?" he asked, frowning as though he couldn't fathom what the word meant.

"Yes. A job. Nine to five. Benefits. All of that. You know, what regular folks do to keep an address."

Kamran remained silent for a few moments as he peered at her.

"How much do they pay you?"

She winced, then flickered a gaze to his right and felt the intensity of everyone's attention. "It doesn't matter."

"How much?" He beckoned for her to come nearer. "Whisper it to me."

Ellena hesitated a moment, then complied, moving so close she inhaled the intoxicating scent of sandalwood. She managed to whisper an answer, then inched back to put a little distance between them.

"For the rest of your life?" he asked, his tone and wide eyes reflecting the incredulity registered in his facial expression.

"Until I'm sixty-seven and retire," she replied, daunted by his tone. "But there's also health benefits and other factors that I can't put a number on."

Kamran blinked as though doing a set of mental calculations and coming up with what probably amounted to simple interest on his bank account. "Give me the particulars and I will wire the money into your account."

She parted her lips to protest but he held up a hand. "Saying yes to taking me as your husband is still your choice. With this, I am simply ensuring your peace of mind. And as a gift for your kindness, your selflessness in saving a child who was a stranger to you."

Ellena let out a long, slow breath, because staying here permanently, marrying him, would be a lost cause. She loved her job as a personal assistant at Vantage Point. Alejandro Reyes, a "Fixer" of everything from political and corporate espionage, to terrorist attacks, was the absolute best person to work for. And she loved the predictability of her life. Traveling overseas was the most adventurous event in her life. Still, curiosity won out over common sense and she said, "All right. Thank you."

"Now we go about the business of getting to know one another," he said, smiling as though her consent brought him much pleasure. Evidently, he wanted this to happen and the intensity of his gaze bore into her soul. "So that you can make an informed decision, yes?"

She glanced over his shoulder, taking in some of the envious looks a few of the women tried to hide. "Why are you doing this?" she asked him. "Why are you allowing them to serve you up to some foreign woman as if you do not have value?"

"Because I recognize this is God's will," he answered. "And who am I to leave a precious gift unwrapped?"

Her eyebrows drew in, as she tried to decipher the hidden meaning behind his words. The man had a peaceful, confident air but also a playful vibe about him.

"Yes, that was a double entendre." His smile widened and she could swear the heavens opened up and smiled with him.

Good Lord, I'm in trouble.

Chapter 2

"You will stay here tonight," the Sheikh commanded. His firm expression dared anyone to question his decision.

"I am here with my classmates." Ellena tore her gaze from Kamran. "We're supposed to see the sights," she protested. "They're probably worried."

"You will be in good hands with Kamran Ali Khan."

"But —"

"Say thank you, Ellena," Kamran whispered, under the Sheikh's fierce frown.

She shifted her gaze to his, saw the warning in his eyes. "Thank you." Then she gave him the Arabic greeting.

The Sheikh flinched, then refocused as he smiled and replied in kind. He slid back onto the throne. "See, she even knows a little Arabic. The proper way to greet. Now your love of Western culture will be put to good use, my son."

"Can he force me to stay here?" she said in Kamran's ear.

"It would be an insult to refuse his hospitality."

"But I don't know any of the customs here—"

"Shhhhh," Kamran whispered, taking her hand in his. "It is fine. You will be fine."

"He can't just throw you away like this," she murmured, searching his eyes for some form of deception. "You don't know me."

Kamran gave her hand a gentle squeeze and guided her to the foyer under the curious gazes of everyone else. "Ellena, nine days is a long time. Today, I will walk you through the palace grounds and then you will give me your original itinerary. I will be certain to take you every place you had planned to see." His dark-brown gaze lasered in on her. "Will that be all right?"

"That sounds nice, but what about the people I was traveling with? This is a class reunion. I haven't seen some of them in ten years. That's the sole purpose of this trip."

"A few inquired at the hospital," Kamran said, walking past the guards at the pathway leading to the exit. "They know you are with the Royal Family. Come, my mother will have a room prepared for you. Tomorrow, we will check into Jumillah."

"What's that?"

"The most precious hotel in Durabia," he said. "And since it is on a private island, it affords the right kind of seclusion."

She nodded, trying to balance herself. All of this was overwhelming.

"Oh, and we are going to the Durabia Mall for you to pick up a few tunics, all right?"

Ellena stopped walking. "What is wrong with …"

"You will be interacting with the Royal Family," he said in a patient tone. "You must cover certain …" He lowered his gaze to the cleavage baring blouse. "*Assets*, accordingly."

She tried to pull away. "It's all too much. It's so fast. What if I make a mistake?"

"You will not. Please do not worry."

Ellena scanned his face again, and could not believe how calm he was, given the circumstances. "Aren't you angry? He just—"

"May I be honest?" he said, and his voice was deep, rich, like the smoothest whiskey.

"Yes. Sure."

"You had me at 'he is still a man. He still has value. A brain, intelligence, and a purpose'."

With that being said, Kamran gave her a slight bow as his mother came forward to guide her into an alcove that led to a suite of rooms. He walked past, leaving Ellena's mind churning in circles.

Chapter 3

"Well, if it isn't our Royal traveler," Dolly teased as Ellena and Kamran made it into the area where her classmates had congregated in the Hyatt's revolving restaurant.

Kamran had called ahead and the front desk informed everyone that breakfast and a meeting would be held around eight. The place had a mix of tables and sofas in green, gold and creams; everything situated so nothing obstructed view of the Durabian skyline.

Accompanying them were Kamran's two bodyguards—Rashid and Waqas, personal assistant, Saqib, along with Saba, the aide they assigned to Ellena to instruct her in palace protocol and to address any needs she might have.

His mother had been more welcoming than Ellena expected, given this culture did not seem to take kindly to interracial marriages.

"My son is a most wonderful, empathic, and enterprising young man," she said. *"Please do not break his heart."*

"That is very premature," Ellena protested. *"He doesn't know me.*

There's a very good chance I won't hold his heart long enough to break it."

"You do not know my son," she said with a warm smile. "He was the one who insisted that you be rewarded for your bravery. And now his reward is a woman who defies his father to defend who he is." She cupped Ellena's face in her hands. "You do not know how much that meant to him and me. I have only wanted for his happiness after his father has caused him so much pain."

"Hey everyone," Ellena said as Kamran whispered something to the guards before closing the distance between them until he was standing next to her.

Damaris, a woman with a warm brown complexion and sharp, angular hairstyle and Dolly, a caramel curvaceous woman, both left their table and came to where Ellena stood. Dolly gave Kamran a lengthy onceover, taking in the white tunic—*dishdasha*—and pants, then his sandals, but she lingered several moments on his face. "Who is this gorgeous man and did they make any more like him?"

"Well, um … he's um …"

"Her royal escort," Kamran supplied with a slight bow.

Kamran's main bodyguard's head whipped around so fast Ellena thought it would fly off. The second one did pretty much the same. Kamran gave both of them a warning glare to instruct them to stand down.

"Damn, woman," Damaris said with a hearty chuckle. "Leave you in the hospital for one day and you've got a fine ass man on your arm. And you're dressed like the Queen of Sheba."

"Does he have a brother?" Dolly teased, grinning like she was about to hit the lottery.

Kamran simply smiled, put his focus on Ellena and said, "Breakfast anyone?"

"So, it's like that, huh?" Damaris shot back with a sour expression as she wagged her finger at him. "I see what you did there."

"First Tailan gets with that movie star," Dolly said. "Now you're hanging out with the head Durabians in charge."

"Tailan is here?" Ellena asked, craning her neck to find her friend.

"What's that?" Carrie demanded, sidling up next to Damaris and nearly crashing into the woman in her zeal to insert herself in the conversation.

Ellena shrank from her caustic tone and the unwanted interruption. Carrie had been a bully since their high school days. She'd made Ellena's life hell simply because she came from a broken, poor family while Carrie was the result of two high-powered lawyers. Carrie could have attended an upscale private school of her choice. However, her lack of effort landed her in public school. She took every opportunity to remind everyone of how superior her life was to that of every other student.

"On your finger," Carrie gestured to the rock that Kamran had placed on Ellena's hand that morning. His actions were meant to signal to the world that for the time being, she was no longer available for any men to approach her. The minute they hit the Free Zone, an area that was less restrictive, attention was immediately drawn to them. Some of the single male classmates they encountered in the lobby weren't feeling the "message" at all. Several had stepped to Ellena and made their desires known. Right in front of Kamran! Soon, his bodyguards had to run interference before Kamran laid someone flat.

"You weren't wearing that when we got here. So, what's up with that?"

Carrie's voice was loud enough to call everyone's attention to the gift he had personally picked out before they arrived at the Hyatt for breakfast. The jewelry store owner opened the place mega-early just for them. Saba, Ellena's new assistant, was now upstairs retrieving her personal effects from the room she was supposed to share with a classmate. One of Kamran's bodyguards was assigned to look out for Ellena. Being royalty did have its privileges.

"A gift from the king," Kamran answered, his gaze narrowing on the slender woman with a face that had graced a few magazine spreads.

"Wow. What a lucky break." The jealousy in Carrie's green eyes was prevalent. If any doubt existed that she meant anything but, the scowl that marred her pretty face said the rest.

Kamran took Ellena's hand in his and pressed a kiss to the ring, causing her to gasp and a sliver of desire to work its way up and down her body.

"Why did you do that?" Ellena whispered so only he could hear.

"To give her something to be extremely angry about."

"Kamran, you can't claim me like this in front of them," she warned, trying to put a bit of distance between them. Little did he know that his action would bring unwanted curiosity. "People will get the wrong idea."

"Which idea?" he challenged, leveling a heated gaze on her. "That you will belong to me?" His warm smile disarmed whatever nuclear barb she planned to launch his way. "Come, you must be famished."

"Kamran …"

"Ellena …" he countered with a megawatt grin. The man was turning on the charm full blast and he knew she was definitely not immune.

Touched that he had picked up on the very thing that would make Carrie so jealous she'd practically explode, Ellena gave him a conspiratorial look. "You are so bad."

"You mean that in a good way, yes?" He wiggled his eyebrows in the most unexpected, comedic fashion and she laughed. "I was thinking that we could have Saba enhance your original itinerary so your group will have a more well-rounded experience."

Her assistant was a bright-eyed Durabian woman that Kamran brought to her room in the palace last night after his mother had settled her in and Kamran returned to kidnap her on that promised tour.

"You mean upgraded?"

He shrugged and didn't make eye contact at first as Ellena avoided the curious glances of her other classmates and their significant others, who were closely watching their interaction. "I am not sure how some of your people will perceive it. I realize you came to explore Durabia with them—and now, I have been added to the equation."

In other words, a compromise was on deck because he wasn't going anywhere.

"They'll get over it," she said. "Let me see what the group organizers have to say." Ellena faced the next table where her friends were chowing down on some of the buffet specialties. "Damaris and Dolly, I need to speak with you for a moment."

They moved away from David, Sheree, Ronnie—all members of the reunion committee, and Dolly put her eyes solely on Kamran. "Sure, what's going on?" Dolly asked.

Kamran explained his thoughts. The two women shared a speaking glance before their faces split in a mile-wide grin. "I'll get a consensus from the group real quick and we can go from there," Damaris said.

Ellena nodded. "Sounds like a plan."

"Yo, listen up!" Damaris bellowed loud enough to cover the distance of the entire restaurant and then some, since their group was the only one present.

Kamran blanched, blinked, and shook his head. Conversations trickled to a halt as everyone's attention settled on Damaris and Dolly who stood near the yogurt station.

"Ellena's royal escort dude wants to upgrade our experience. What say you?"

"What the hell does that mean?" Carrie shot back, voicing the sentiments of the sour-faced crew sitting at the table with her. Former "pretty girls" who hung with Carrie and the men from the football and basketball teams.

"It means we get better accommodations at no additional cost," Dolly replied, her frustration with the homecoming queen—and the fact that half of the people on this reunion trip sided with her for everything—evident. Same way it was in high school. Old habits didn't die hard, they had an afterlife too. "Notice we now have this entire restaurant to ourselves every morning. The buffet wasn't part of our original package, either. You're already benefiting from his hospitality, so quit being all extra."

Dolly stepped forward. "Show of hands. Upgraded with Ellena and the royal dude?"

Half of the hands went up.

"Keep things as they are?" Damaris said in a tone that clearly showed how stupid she thought that choice would be.

The other fifty percent shot their hands in the air.

"All right. It's split." Dolly grimaced before focusing on Kamran "What are we going to do, because I'm rolling with you."

Kamran scanned the faces of everyone. "Those who are … rolling with Ellena, step this way."

Ellena gestured to her assistant to come forward. "Saba, please take their names. Give them to Kamran when you're done."

The woman with a meek demeanor and bright smile, complied and a few people came over to embrace Ellena before she stood aside, allowing them to give their full names and room numbers.

"It is about fifty and two people," Saba said to Kamran when she was done. "With us, and your entourage, that will be a full busload."

Kamran nodded, then to the people around him he asked, "Does everyone have WhatsApp on their cell?"

Some shook their heads, others nodded.

"It will work on the hotel's signal, so I need you to download it right now and add these two numbers," he said before relaying his personal number and also the one to his assistant. "Before we leave the hotel, you will have the new itinerary and any reminders or changes can be sent through to everyone at once."

Saba glided forward and showed him the list as everyone went back to their meals.

Kamran held out his hand and his guard, Rashid, placed a cell in his palm. He then gathered all the current incoming calls into a "group", then typed a single message and sent it to everyone's phone at the same time.

Soon, the persons with the Kamran and Ellena group held their hands in the air, signaling that they received what he sent.

"Hands down," he said. "Our bus will be here directly after breakfast to take everyone to Gold Souk and Spice Souk. We will also visit the Durabia Museum. That will be about sixty minutes from now."

Kamran then whispered something to Saqib that Ellena couldn't quite catch.

"What are you up to?" she asked as his assistant practically skipped away, smiling.

"No good." He lifted an eyebrow playfully in an unexpected manner, causing her to laugh. "I want to make sure the outing is enjoyable for you and your friends."

This man right here. He is playing for keeps.

Chapter 4

One hour later, both groups filed through the Hyatt's side lobby entrance and out to the buses. But a marked difference existed between the modes of transport. Ellena's group had a luxury vehicle awaiting. The rest were rolling in one that paled by comparison. Grumbles of discontent echoed among those who hadn't chosen the upscale experience. As Ellena's classmates tipped by them on their way to the bus Kamran had commissioned, he personally handed each of them a sealed envelope and asked that they wait to open them.

"What's in those?" Ellena queried with a nod towards her classmates.

"You will see."

She folded her arms across her breasts as the last passenger boarded. "Are you keeping secrets from me already?"

"No, my love … no," he quickly corrected and took a deep breath as though wondering if he had overstepped a boundary. "It is only a surprise. Nothing more."

That endearment slipped past his lips all too quickly, but something about those words warmed her heart. *My love*.

The bus pulled off and Ellena and Kamran settled in their seats. He extracted the microphone from its cradle on the dashboard and said, "Good Morning, everyone. Let me explain a little bit about Gold Souk. This is a place where you bargain. They will give you the highest price first. Remember they are all there to make money. Your job is to get the best price possible. You do not know what that is until you walk away and then they say 'okay, I will give it to you for …'—that is a better offer, but still probably not the best. Throw out something lower than what they actually accept and see what happens. Decide if it is important or if you believe someone else will sell it at a lower cost." He held up a sampling of paper currency. "Remember Durabian currency is three-and-a-half of what the American dollar brings."

"Can we open the envelopes, Kamran?" Sheree asked, her grin wide enough to cover the length of the bus.

"Not yet. Give it time." Everyone groaned as he reclaimed his seat next to Ellena. He leaned toward her. "Your people are so impatient."

"So am I."

He stroked her hand and looked into her eyes. "Trust me."

She arched one brow. "I don't even know you enough to do that."

"You will," he whispered, and those words touched someplace deep inside.

They arrived at an open area with riverboats, yachts, and the Durabia skyline as a backdrop across from the beginning stretch of land called the Gold Souk.

"*Now* you can open your envelopes."

Before he finished the sentence, a collective rip of paper echoed through the bus.

"Whoa!" was followed by a roar of joy, squeals, and excitement so loud Ellena had to cover her ears.

"Just something to get you started." He pointed a warning finger at them, looking more like a school librarian than a man who was from a Royal line. "Do not spend it all in one place. We will meet back here in two hours before we move on."

"My man." Ronnie put his hands out for a pound—a fist bump—and Kamran was only too happy to oblige.

"So where is my envelope?" Ellena asked, frowning, but before he could answer, Dolly made it to the front of the bus and asked, "What exact time are we supposed to be back?"

"Two hours from now will mean being back here at eleven sharp," Kamran answered, sweeping his gaze across everyone. "The bus will leave, and if you miss it, you can take a cab back to the hotel."

"My envelope?" Ellena asked sweetly.

"You don't need one," he replied, stroking the underside of her arm. "You have me."

"And what does that mean?" she countered, giving him a long look. "I can trade you in for gold?"

A mysterious smile accompanied his words. "Soon you will know."

They stopped at the first-tier shopping places along the riverfront, bustling with other tourists. Kamran remained silent as Ellena negotiated for pashminas—colorful silk or cashmere scarves—shot glasses, and refrigerator magnets. She felt buoyed by his encouraging smiles but didn't miss the fact that he actually paid more than the final asking amount. "Why have me do all that work if you're going to pay the higher amount?"

"They know I come from the Royal Family," he answered, forking over some currency. "I cannot, in good conscience, pay them bargain prices."

"But you didn't pay what they asked for the first time."

One of the vendors nodded as though to say, *Yes, what she said.*

"And I did not say I was foolish either," he countered, shutting the man and Ellena down. "Only half of what they threw out there is a viable cost. This way, any time you come, they will remember you were with me and treat you at least halfway decent."

Ellena laughed at his clever actions. "My mother used to say, 'you can be a fool, but don't be a *damn* fool'."

"Tell me about her," Kamran insisted, his eyes leveling on her.

All humor drained from her like water through a sieve. Her shoulders slumped and she shifted her feet. Ellena felt small and ... vulnerable. Her physical reaction mirrored exactly how she felt.

"I... I..." She shrugged and couldn't seem to move another step. The weight of the estranged relationship descended on her, along with the reason it existed.

"Too painful?" he asked, concern instantly flashing in his eyes. "Is she ... gone?"

"No, she's alive, but she shouldn't be," she said with bitterness lacing her tone. "Not after what she did to me."

Kamran waved the bodyguards away. The two men put only a little distance between them. But they also kept their focus on Ellena as though sensing the change in her as well. "We do not have to talk about this right now."

Ellena's tear-filled gaze locked on him. "She killed all four of my children."

Chapter 5

Kamran quickly overcame his shock and drew a trembling Ellena into his arms. He held her close to his heartbeat. "Oh, my love, I am so sorry that happened to you." He guided her past the shops and across the street, back to where the bus waited as the guards juggled their packages, struggling to keep up their hurried pace.

"Driver, we need some privacy here." He passed some currency to Rashid. "Bring her two bottles of Croissiere. And I would like two bottles of Hafsa. Then buy something nice, whatever you like, for yourself and whoever else you would like."

"Sir, I am not supposed to leave you unguarded," Rashid protested. "Your father will have my head."

Waqas nodded as he added, "You know security of a Royal is a serious matter."

The two men who were tall, beefy, and well groomed, could pass for twins—mostly on their menacing aura and demeanor alone.

"Then trade off," Kamran shot back, cradling Ellena in his arms. "Go one at a time, but everyone will stay outside of the bus while we talk. Understood?"

"Yes, sir." The driver did a little skip, then came back, a little flushed from just that short stint in the heat. "So, half of that is mine, right?"

Kamran glanced at Rashid, who had been with him the longest. "Three ways."

"I will be back," Rashid said to Waqas, who took up a post in front of the door. The driver gave a sheepish smile and followed Rashid to the walkway that would take them across the street.

Kamran didn't miss the fact that his guard said something to the driver that made him miss a step.

* * *

Kamran settled on the front seat beside Ellena and waited several moments while she gained her bearings.

"I shouldn't do this," she whispered, trying to pull back from him. "Just put this all out there so early in this … this whatever it is."

"This is *perfect* time," he countered, stroking his fingers across her cheek to remove some of the tears. "I cannot know you, if I do not understand your pain. It is also a part of you. And as your mate, this is something that you should not feel that you must hide."

She pulled away to look up at him. "My mate?"

"And out of all of that, that is the only thing you took away," he teased.

"My mate?" she repeated, tilting her head.

"Speaking it into existence," he said with a small smile and she actually gave him one in return.

Ellena then inhaled and placed her head on the wall of his chest. "I was married for seven years. My ex … it was an ugly divorce. So ugly that he moved to a different state. Just up and did that out of the blue. He wore me down so hard before the proceedings even started that I gave up everything except wanting something for the children." She took another deep breath and let it out slowly. "He moved because he was going to start the real proceedings in that particular state then planned to take my children so he wouldn't have to pay me a dime. The judge in Chicago wasn't having it, so my ex stalled things until he came up with another plan." She gazed out at the river, taking in the sight of the ships sailing parallel to the Gold Souk area. "My mother was always money hungry …"

And that was putting it mildly. Like several of her eleven children, Ruth Hinton had also managed to manipulate their only brother into allowing her to handle his finances. She juggled payments between her bills and his until things became so bad that she missed a few of his car payments and was too afraid to tell him what she'd done. She couldn't make arrangements because it would require explaining her error, and of course she wouldn't admit she made so much of a mistake. He only found out the day he went outside, planning to make it to work that morning and his car was gone. Repossessed. He had been complicit and allowed her to have that level of control to hide his assets from his children's mother. It worked, until it didn't.

"So it wasn't too farfetched to believe that Ruth would take my ex-husband's money as part of a deal that would line her pockets at my expense. Not to mention the time that she outright stole bail money destined for one of my sisters, which resulted in an unfortunate and unwarranted stay in a Mississippi prison that led to more tragic experiences." Ellena blinked away tears. "She picked the children up from school, without my permission, and was taking them to live with him," Ellena said, gripping the edge of the barrier railing. "They had an accident."

Kamran's heart constricted and he slid one arm around her.

"Ruth was texting him to let him know they were at the halfway point. She didn't brake fast enough mid-way through a red light and an eighteen-wheeler slammed into her car. None of my children were in seatbelts. She was, but they weren't."

Ellena put a tighter grip on his hand. "One of my babies died instantly. The others died within a few days of each other. My mother survived," she scoffed and grimaced. "Of all the people for God to take, He left her trifling ass and took my babies. All four of them."

Kamran leaned over and grabbed a tissue from the dashboard to wipe her tears as Rashid put an array of packages under the bus then switched places with Waqas. The driver grinned and gave him a thumbs up sign. Rashid gave the man a warning with a hand gesture and the driver's smile disappeared.

"Do you know what their father said to me?"

Kamran shook his head, tightening his hold on her body.

"Now we can stop fighting over them," she spat. "God … God's got them."

Kamran's heart slammed against his chest. What a horrible thing to say about such a tragedy.

"God's got them." She dabbed her face with the tissue. "I did everything right. Waited until I had walked down the aisle to have sex. Kept a clean house, cooked breakfast and dinner every day, packed lunches. Gave him whatever he wanted, even when I was so tired from work that I didn't feel like it. Even things I didn't feel comfortable doing. Even when I knew something wasn't right for us financially, he wouldn't listen. I submitted as the Good Book said a wife is supposed to do."

She shook her head "And how does life repay me? God's got 'em, then leaves my ex and my mother with absolutely no consequences for what they did. The judge said that losing the children was punishment enough, even though their deception was the root cause."

She inhaled sharply and Kamran ran one hand up and down her arm to give comfort.

"No more talk of this right now," he whispered into her hair. "Thank you for unburdening your soul."

He cradled her in his arms for a long while, watched when Waqas trotted back to the bus and took his place beside Rashid. The driver took off again in a schoolboy run that signaled his glee.

Kamran would tread carefully when it came to questions about her family. He couldn't imagine the depth of sorrow that still plagued her. "There is nothing I can say that will ease your pain and I am sorry that I brought you to this state."

"It's not your fault," she said, sniffling, then accepted the rest of the tissues from his hand. "You couldn't have known. Just hormones are all over the place. Early menopause or whatever. Sorry for blubbering like an idiot."

"You are not an idiot," he protested.

"But I am blubbering though."

"Yes, there is that," he agreed. "But with good reason. Tears are orgasms for the eyes."

She pulled away and gave him the side-eye. "You just made that up."

"No, I promise. I read it somewhere," he said with a laugh. "But it is true? You feel a little better right now, yes? A release?"

Ellena blinked, and those perfectly arched eyebrows drew in. "Truthfully, I do. Yes."

"I want you to close your eyes and take a deep breath in."

She took a moment, then complied.

"Now let it out slowly."

Ellena did, and he guided her through the process eight more times. When she was done, she buried her head in the wall of his muscled chest once again. He was glad she was comfortable enough to relax to this degree.

"Honey?"

"Yes, Kamran."

His gaze shifted to one of the side windows. "Your classmates are returning."

"All right," she whispered.

"I thought you did not want them to know."

"I don't care." She held onto him and he placed a gentle kiss on her forehead.

"Are you sure?"

"Yes."

He signaled for the driver to come aboard but Rashid stepped on right after, doing a sweep of the bus before giving the driver a sign and allowing her classmates to step inside.

"See, I told you there was love in the air," Dolly teased, nudging Damaris as they walked past.

Kamran smiled, but did not feel the need to respond.

"Oh, so it's like that?" David said with a nod. "Royal escort, my ass."

Kamran took the microphone after everyone was accounted for. "So, would you prefer to go on to the museum or stay here for more shopping?"

"I opt for shopping," Dolly replied and several affirming nods and verbal agreements followed. "Only if we can see the museum another day?"

Damaris chimed in, "I'd like to get it in while the merchants still remember the prices they gave us."

"But some of us need to change clothes and shoes," Dolly said, sliding off her heels and rubbing her aching feet. "This weather and that walk ain't nothing nice."

Kamran directed his focus to the driver first, then to everyone else. "So Ellena and I will retire to Jumillah and this bus will take you to the hotel to change and drop off packages. Then you will come back here for more shopping. Plan?"

Everyone agreed.

"But then get some rest," he cautioned. "I have a surprise for you tonight. Includes dinner so bring a healthy appetite."

"Another envelope?" Ronnie prompted.

"You might think I was raised a fool, but I was not raised a damn fool."

Ellena squinted, grimaced, then let out a peal of laughter before everyone joined in.

"Oh, man, he's hella cool," Damaris said.

"On the way back to Gold Souk, the driver will give you a tour of the city. Everyone should buy something for a trip to the Grand Mosque in Abu Dhabi that will take place sometime this week." He put his focus on Dolly and Damaris. "I will need you to set the time in my absence." Then to everyone else, he said, "The bus will pick you up from the hotel tonight at six. Not CP time, yes?"

"What the hell do you know about CP time?" Ronnie challenged him on the term that mean "Colored People's time".

"It will be the difference between making it to my next surprise or remaining at the hotel."

Hoots and laughter met that statement.

"And dress up," he said, giving Ellena's hand a gentle squeeze. "No jeans or anything casual."

Dolly piped up. "You're not going to tell us?"

"How can it be a surprise if you know?" he shot back with a wink. "But I promise you will love it."

Ellena splayed a hand on his chest. "You can tell me, though, right?"

"No can do." He tweaked the tip of her nose. "Surprise is for you, too."

"You are such a tease."

Kamran tipped his head sideways. "You mean that in a good way, yes?"

Chapter 6

The bus pulled up in front of a two-lane pathway leading to an island with only one building—a sprawling glass structure shaped like a ship's sail. Ellena and Kamran stepped off with a farewell to everyone.

"Wait, where are y'all going?" Dolly called out, getting to her feet.

"Ellena needs a little rest and to prepare for tonight."

"Be honest, y'all going up there for a little pickle tickle," Damaris teased.

Kamran looked at Ellena. "Pickle tickle?"

"Yes, it is exactly what you think," she confirmed.

His eyes widened with shock. "Oh. Definitely not for that. Too short of a time."

Ellena playfully shoved him in the side as everyone laughed at them.

Ronnie leaned over to peer out of the window. "You're staying here?"

"Yes, for the duration of the vacation," Kamran answered, placing his hand in the small of Ellena's back.

"Man, that's tight. So, when do we check in? You know, an upgrade and everything."

"See you all tonight," Kamran said as his guards alighted from the bus to where Saba and Saqib awaited. "Remember, make sure you all purchase something to wear to the Mosque tomorrow. Your driver will explain what that is."

"Oh, he's good," David said. "Just slid right by that question."

"That's 'cause you need to keep your nose out of their business," Dolly warned.

* * *

Kamran waved as the bus pulled away. "Are you all right?" he asked as they walked along the concrete path leading to the entrance of Jumillah Hotel. Guards walked a few paces behind them.

"Yes, I'm good." Seconds passed before she glanced up at him. "Why did you separate me from the group?"

"You need to rest," he said, pausing to allow her to look in his eyes. "Your experience, telling me what happened in your past, that was draining and you still need some time to process. Shopping can wait. A little libation and a meal, and some rest before tonight, yes?"

"You are so good to me," she whispered, cupping his face in her hands. "I'm going to be so spoiled. I don't ever want to …"

He pressed a kiss to her lips and quickly pulled back, startled at his own actions, but not regretful. "And that is my point. But this break is not for that reason, it is because you still need to heal from your past. What your mother did … that kind of betrayal. I can almost place money on the fact that you have never opened up to anyone else about it."

Ellena averted her gaze, but not for long. She looked up at him, as though trying to read his true intentions. He had been truthful when he said she'd had his heart on day one. That feisty spirit, that passion was … sexy. Yes, sexy. That's what they termed it. Everything about the woman was so different than what he was used to.

Jumillah Hotel, a sky-high palace, was situated on an island off to itself. The suite had classical furnishings with beautiful views of the pale blue waters and the Durabian skyline. They entered through a private lift that led straight into a cinema, library, dining room for twelve, and a fully stocked kitchen where a butler, housekeeper and assistant awaited to provide personal service fit for a king.

The tranquil waters flowing around the hotel could be seen through cathedral windows. Two grand and luxurious bedrooms had his and hers dressing rooms and two private bars. Both master bathrooms came complete with a full-size Jacuzzi and a separate five-head rain shower as well as a set of his and hers Hermès amenities, and another guest restroom on the lower level.

She tipped into the bedroom and found a selection of nine types of pillows, eiderdown duvets, exquisite Egyptian cotton linen and a bed that could be personalized to suit her specific posture preferences.

"I will leave you to your rest," he said. "Saba will take care of your packages and gifts. I will be staying in the suite right above this one."

"Stay with me," she whispered, then inched back as though shocked she had issued such an invitation.

He turned back to face her. "Are you certain?"

"Yes," she gestured to the spread on the dining room table. "There's enough food here for two."

Kamran walked past her to one of the chairs and pulled it out, waiting. She took her seat and he claimed the one next to her.

They shared a meal of Al Machboos—bismati rice, onions, and chicken seasoned with spices, salt, and dried lemon; Tabbouleh—a salad made from tomatoes, green onions and cucumber, seasoned with fresh mint and lemon juice; Baba ganoush—smoked eggplant mixed with onions, tomatoes, and olive oil; Shish Tawook—a beef and lamb kabob, along with several other delicacies. All the while, they enjoyed light banter and conversation about her classmates, time in high school, and a little of her life. He fired questions at her so fast she didn't get to ask him too much.

"Now you must rest," he said after a final bite. "I will see you tonight."

"All right." She stood along with him.

Kamran made it as far as the door.

"Would it be bold of me to ask you to stay? Again."

He was by her side in an instant, slipping off the dishdasha, taking off his sandals, then removing his head covering—*Iqal*—placing it across the chair before allowing her to guide him into the bedroom. What remained was a thin pair of pants and a bright-white t-shirt that clung to his muscular chest. The man had the nerve to have a six pack.

He slid into the bed and gathered Ellena in his arms. She was asleep before he could say sweet dreams.

Chapter 7

Durabia Opera House, a performing arts center, was located in the heart of downtown. The place hosted a variety of performances and events including theatre, opera, ballet, concerts, conferences, and exhibitions. The vibrant colors of gold and black were infused throughout, but the glass structure held elements of class and mystery.

"Wow, you're taking us to some boring ass opera?" Ronnie said, his sour tone signaling exactly how he felt about that prospect.

"First, we'll have a private dinner, then it will be time for my surprise."

Ellena watched as her classmates basked in all the attention showered upon them by the staff because, once again, Kamran had reserved the entire place for their dining pleasure. He looked dashing in a black tux and tie. The other half of their classmates were on a riverboat cruise and a few people had texted to Damaris that the food and entertainment was subpar. Kamran, on the other hand, had made sure his guests were dining on some of the finest cuisine in Durabia. Whatever surprise he had in store, Ellena believed it was going to be epic.

"El, are you all right?" Dolly asked, the red silky dress hugging her curves like they were an old friend.

"Never better." Her gaze drifted until Kamran was in her line of sight. He looked back and winked. She inhaled and her breath caught in her chest. That man oozed every ounce of charm available on the planet. And it was natural—every bit of it. Their conversations as they made ready to leave for tonight had ranged from a few tidbits about his family, a dabble in politics, a little of religion and customs, but a great deal of it focused on hopes and dreams.

"That man is so fine, girl." Dolly nudged Ellena to capture her attention and she complied by tearing her gaze from his. "You should see the way he looks at you."

Ellena found a pointed interest in the plush carpet.

"And that blush," Dolly teased. "Oh my stars, you've *never* blushed. And I'm telling you that the heat between you two is enough to start a fire in this desert." She laughed, and Ellena tried not to give anything else away. The more she spent time with him, the more she realized his mother had been correct. Attentive. Compassionate. Intelligent. Wonderful.

"You know the others are jealous, right? Now Carrie and her people want to have a private talk with Kamran. They were sitting around the lobby when we came through with all those bags. You should've seen their faces. My petty was top level."

Ellena peered at Dolly, frowning. "What did you do?"

"Told them that Kamran gave us a nice amount of dancing cash. Enough that it paid for our entire trip and then some. The jaw drops were epic." She did a little shimmy to express her excitement.

"Keep it up, and they're going to beat you up and take your stuff," she warned.

"I'd like to see them try." Dolly assumed a fake fighting stance that made Ellena laugh. "I'll pull out that Chicago South Side so quick, they won't know what hit them." She zeroed in on Kamran and nodded so Ellena would look his way. "What is he like?"

What was Kamran Ali Kahn, like? Honestly, there was so much he wanted to do here in Durabia but the restrictions that came with his status made that impossible. Sometimes she saw the sadness in his eyes when he stared at the downtown skyline.

"He is ... he is amazing." She locked gazes with Kamran across the room. The intensity of his eyes caused heat to wash over her. "And he's genuine. I don't think any of what he does is an act."

Dolly touched Ellena's hand. "So, what's the real deal with that ring?"

"I made the mistake of joking that I didn't have a husband and the Sheikh offered Kamran Ali Khan as a gift."

Dolly's head whipped to him, where he was now engrossed in a conversation with the men in their group. David and Ronnie mostly dominated the exchange. "So, they're just giving out rich good-looking men with bodies like that, all willy-nilly, huh?"

"Special circumstances."

"Girl, I need to tumble my ass on a conveyor belt my damn self. You were lucky. Two more seconds and it would've been me landing that man." She shook her head. "Never seen a woman move all four cheeks and a couple of chins like that."

Ellena tried to hold in a laugh. "I didn't think. I simply reacted."

"Well, it paid off big time, didn't it? And I am not going to lie. I'm a whole lot of happy for you, but just a wee tiny bit jealous, though."

Dolly had always been known for her kind heart and level head. In freshman year, she alone spearheaded a campaign that raised money for a classmate whose family was burned out of their home.

"Question," Ellena said. "Should I be worried?"

"No girl. That's just human nature kicking in." Her gaze wandered to the bodyguard on Kamran's right, who was trying—unsuccessfully—not to lay eyes on Dolly's lush curves. "Besides, Rashid is more my speed. But I am going to give you a piece of unsolicited advice."

Ellena looked her way.

"If you're able to find one iota of happiness with that man, take it." She placed her hand over Ellena's. "I know what you've been through. You deserve any good thing that comes your way. You feel me?"

"I do," she whispered.

"Come, everyone." Kamran beckoned them to dispatch from all areas of the restaurant to the elevators. "You will take the lift down to the first level where one of the guides will direct you to our designated seats."

Ellena left Dolly and slid up to him, whispering, "You're enjoying this?"

"It is not often that I am able to be a host," he said, favoring her with a heated glance. "Yes, I am enjoying all of this."

"And you're not going to tell me what we're about to get into?"

Waiting for the lift to return, he leaned closer to murmur in her ear, causing Ellena to perk up. Then he simply placed a kiss on her lips that sent shivers of pleasure down her spine. He pulled away, watching her reaction to his gentle caress. Desire smoldered in his eyes and she had to force herself to look away to get her bearings.

"That was so unfair."

Kamran extended his arm, and she released a steadying breath. Ellena hooked her arm under his as he guided her into one of the empty lifts once the doors opened.

An attendant beckoned them to approach an entrance where her classmates were congregated. "Your seats are at the front, near the stage."

"Thank you," Kamran said.

Dolly caught up with her. "Wow, top-flight all the way." Then did a little two-step in her long dress.

"Opera? Really?" David griped to Kamran with a sarcastic tone as Ronnie nodded, looking like he'd eaten sour grapes for breakfast, lunch, and dinner. "I'm about to get my snooze on."

Kamran smiled in that self-satisfied way, which made her give him a side-eye. Every poster or advertisement had been covered with silk cloths. When they made it to their reserved seats, instead of a full orchestra and instruments on stage, a keyboard, drum set, and three microphones were situated there.

"Did he tell you?" Dolly asked Ellena in a low enough tone that Kamran couldn't hear.

"No, he's keeping me in the dark, too."

"Damn, I'm so curious," she said, sighing.

The rest of the crowd came in and settled in the areas behind them. The drummer, bassist, and lead guitar players along with a keyboardist took their places. They were followed by two singers with ivory skin and long dark hair that complimented their tea-length black gowns.

"I don't ever remember an opera with this kind of set up."

Kamran chuckled and he stroked her hand but kept his focus on the stage.

"And tonight," a voice bellowed several minutes later. "Durabia Opera House says welcome to Mica Paris."

The audience erupted in cheers and applause.

"Who?" Dolly piped in.

"One Temptation," Ellena offered the name of the artist's major hit song. "Breathe Life Into Me."

Damaris leaned forward so she could see past Dolly. "Oh, she sings opera now?"

"Something is telling me this is not the traditional opera," Ellena answered, unable to miss the smirk on Kamran's face as he still wouldn't give up the goods.

"Change of plans, people," Mica Paris said, sauntering out on the stage to another roar of applause. The songstress had creamy dark skin, wore a floor-length black gown fitted with a cape about the shoulders; a cap of ebony curls framed her angular face.

"They flew me in for one show but looks like I'll be doing a late night after this one." She scanned the area closest to the stage. "Is Kamran Ali Khan in the house?"

Kamran raised his hand.

"Thank you for your kind offer," she said, beaming down at him, then leaned out to shake his hand. "This Jamaican girl can put away a whole lot of jerk chicken for that kind of dunsai."

Laughter trickled through the audience as she settled the mic in the right position and glanced over her shoulder to make sure everyone in her band was in place. "First, y'all, I'm about to take you to church. This tribute to Aretha Franklin is a nod to the Queen of Soul. Put away your cell phones and cameras. Thanks to Sheikh Kamran, there is no need to record this experience."

Ellena was familiar with a few Mica Paris tunes but didn't realize she had the singing chops to pull Aretha off. Mica's voice had that smoky, sexy sound more reminiscent of Sara Vaughn than the Queen of Soul.

The room grew eerily silent. Mica hit the first notes of *Amazing Grace*, and Ellena gripped the hand rest. The song struck a deep chord within.

Kamran lifted her hand to his lips and said, "Enjoy, my love."

Chapter 8

A tear streamed down Ellena's face before others joined it at her chin. Kamran kept his hold on her hand, squeezing it to show support for whatever she was feeling.

He was aware that Aretha's songs captured a good range of female experiences and emotions. He had taken a chance, having Saba and Saqib contact Mica's management team to make a request to provide this special experience for Ellena and her people, then flew her in earlier from Great Britain.

"I can't be Aretha," Mica confessed between the verse and chorus. "There is only one Aretha, but I promise to do my best to honor her the best way I know how. Y'all with me?"

Kamran tucked a few strands of Ellena's hair behind her ear so he could clearly see her face. She closed her eyes, letting the words and the music flow over her. Towards the end of the song, she lifted her gaze to the stage.

Soon the tempo changed into the classic *I Say a Little Prayer for You*. Her classmates in the front area, rocked side to side and snapped their fingers with the beat. The audience sang along before transitioning into *Respect* and *Rock Steady*. The song choices were stellar. Only when the band lit up with *Freeway of Love* did the concert hit a glitch.

The audience was on their feet giving Mica some major love. But something was off. Mica felt it, too. She held up a hand. The band and the background singers faded to a halt. So did the audience.

"Why are they"—she gestured to the audience—"giving me more energy than you are?" Then she put one hand on her hip and Dolly said, "Whoops."

"Let's try this again," Mica demanded. "Come on, now."

The band took a moment to regroup, and then struck up the song again, this time with a noticeable difference. Mica took the mic and they went *in!*

Everyone in the Opera House—from all ethnic backgrounds—was on their feet rocking and grooving, and Ellena noticed that Kamran had rhythm. *Hmmmm, very promising.*

The set went through *Think, Something He Can Feel, Dr. Feelgood, A Natural Woman*, before sliding into a duet with special guest McFarland who crooned *Gotta Find Me an Angel.*

"What do you know about Aretha Franklin?" Ellena asked.

"Her voice is magical," he whispered. "Gladys, Luther, Chaka, even Prince are all on my playlist." He glanced at her. "That surprises you?"

"It does," she confirmed. "Is that what your father meant about your love of Western Culture?"

"Maybe."

The audience was still cheering after the stage had been clear for several minutes. Suddenly, the band strolled back out and the applause was deafening. Mica followed and slid straight into *Jump to It*. The audience. The love. That musical stride. Everything was on point.

When the show was over, the guides directed Kamran, Ellena, and their guests to an area backstage to meet the star and take pictures before the next show.

Mica embraced Kamran warmly. "Only you could get me to do two shows in one night." Then she peered at Ellena. "So, who's the special woman that you needed to fly me in for?"

"Ellena, meet Mica. Mica meet Ellena, my … beloved."

Mica's eyebrow went up as she favored Ellena with a glance. "A sister, huh? Well, I shouldn't be surprised."

"I love your work," Ellena said, trying to ascertain what the artist meant by that.

Mica gave her a megawatt smile. "See, I love her already."

"Seriously," Ellena admitted, chuckling. "The House remix of *Breathe Life Into Me*."

"You're from Chicago?" Mica asked, peering at her closely.

"The House Music capital of the world."

"So glad you could come," Kamran said, as Rashid tapped his watch to signal they had to keep it moving. "And, I owe you one."

Mica nodded. "Although, I think that second crowd is going to be asleep before I start. How are you going to feed them to keep them happy because they have to wait?"

Reality slammed into Ellena. "Wait a minute, you had them add a show and push the people who were supposed to be in this show to another time?"

"Yes," he answered.

"Why not just have a private show somewhere else?"

"Because the feeling, the sound with all the people here, is a different type of atmosphere than with a private show. I wanted you to see what the opera house offers. Especially since it's part of a major decision for you."

She totally understood. The crowd had been a mix of White, Asian, Middle Eastern people. Ellena and her classmates were the only Blacks in the house. But the fact he understood the nuances of vibration meant so much on a deeper level. Eight days left before she had to give his father that decision. Things were certainly off to a great start.

"Thank you so much."

"My pleasure," he said. "Always." His smile gave him such an elated air she could almost imagine what he had looked like as a little boy.

"Are you trying to make me fall in love with you?"

"Is it working?" he said, and his voice was so serious she could barely formulate an answer.

The bodyguard came up holding a package, which he handed to Mica. "Could you put an autograph on these?"

Ellena did a mental count and realized one thing. "Those are recordings of her performance?"

Before he could answer, Sherelle, one of Carrie's friends who had managed to break ranks on day one and land the last spot available with the Kamran group, slithered in. She had been reporting back to Carrie with everything that transpired with Ellena's group. She parted her lips to say something, but glanced down at Ellena's left hand. Then looked up to lock gazes with Ellena who simply tilted her head, waiting.

"Um, I, um," she stuttered. "Thank you, Sheikh." Then scurried away.

Kamran's gaze followed the woman's hasty retreat. "What was that all about?"

"It's almost after midnight?"

"And?" he prompted, putting his focus on Ellena.

"My grandmother said it's the time when inhibitions and common sense are at an all-time low and you're supposed to have your ass in the house."

"Why?"

"Because nothing is open that late except the emergency room, liquor stores, and legs." She gave him a knowing smile. "Guess which one she was about to offer you?"

Chapter 9

That next morning, Kamran stepped out of a black SUV outside of the Hyatt and was met with a resounding applause and cheers from everyone.

"I'm still on a high from that concert," Dolly said, embracing him. "Thank you. And thank you for that DVD."

Damaris ambled up to his other side and also embraced him as he said, "It was my pleasure."

David offered his fist for a pound. "Who knew we had to travel to the Middle East in order to hear some good old-fashioned R&B?"

Kamran tapped his fist to David's then Ronnie's, who was a concert producer and had a handle on a great deal of talent back in the States.

"So where are we going today, Crown Royal?"

Kamran frowned.

"Outside joke," Ellena said giving Ronnie the evil eye, causing him to chuckle.

Ellena laid her head on his shoulder. She was a little weary because last night they stayed up late with him asking her questions about her life, trying to make sure he knew as much about her as possible. He was an open book, and it took a long while before she finally opened up enough to have the deepest conversation she'd ever had with anyone in her entire life. Being with him had made her reflect on her experiences and how they had made her the woman she was today.

"When I was a little girl," then she laughed and added, *"Don't you love confessions that start that way?"*

His lips lifted at the corners and she could swear that all the charm poured right out of him and into her.

"I wasn't taught to love myself. I wasn't taught what "self" was. I was a child in a home with a mother who didn't want me. I was a sister in a home with a brother who always tried to protect me from my mother's rage. I am sister to nine other girls, only two of them I have a relationship with right now. The others are so toxic that I haven't spoken to them, my mother or brother in years." She glanced down at their joined hands. *"I was a student who only knew that I was supposed to be in school because that's what a child did. But who was self? Who was Ellena Kiley? I existed. I did what I was told. I moved when I was told to move. I lived for acceptance and praise from those who did not show signs that they would hurt me."*

Kamran took her hand in his, a gesture he did all too often and she was beginning to take great comfort in.

"Teachers were pure gold. Recently, I've realized that I might have left the classroom, but my teachers have come in a different form—people in my immediate circle. See, you don't let strangers get close. You don't let co-workers get close. Sometimes, you don't even let family close. But others that you love, you are open and unguarded—and therefore ... vulnerable when you least expect it.

"Even now, as an adult, I struggle with identifying self. Self has

been attached to survivor, auntie, mentor, and a few things that tip on the negative side. But when I was married, something else came to light that I had not ever considered. Too giving, too caring, not protective of my emotional health, not protective of my physical well-being, not protective of my mental health, not protective of my financial health, not protective of ... self." She inhaled, using one of his techniques, and let it out slowly. "I'm telling you that sometimes a person comes along and blatantly introduces you to a part of self that sends you into reflection. The whole 'who am I, what is my purpose thing'." She locked gazes with him and there was a sadness in her eyes that was so profound, he wanted to curl her into his arms and never let her go. "Why do I invite or keep people into my life who can hurt me on a level so deep that it makes me question why I do the things I do for others?"

"Because it takes a while to master the art of self-preservation," Kamran explained, and she realized that on some level he had done the same. From what he had told her earlier, his brothers warranted the distance he had given them, same as with her own family. They shared that in common. She could count on her left hand how many family members with which she had any dealings.

"We tend to overlook that," he continued. "We give to others—time, money—opportunities—sometimes because it's in our nature and it's part of who we are. Sometimes that giving takes more from self than we have to give. We don't recognize it until what's supposed to be our normal self has hit a mental, emotional, and physical pain threshold and we realize we've absorbed a blow that wouldn't have happened if we were self-aware. That's when regret sets in." He gave her hand an encouraging squeeze. "That's when kicking ourselves sets in. That's when realizing 'self' had already given you a warning that you didn't heed, hence ..." He simply shrugged but his words let her know that he knew exactly what she felt inside.

They shared the same thoughts on a number of things and she fell asleep in his arms, and was reluctant to let go when Rashid came to make sure they made it to the Hyatt on time.

Eighteen black SUVs pulled up to the hotel that morning to take Ellena, Kamran, and her classmates to the sand dunes and for a night at the oasis. Not at midnight like Minnie Ripperton sang about, but close enough. The rest of the classmates where shuttled into traditional all-terrain Jeeps that did not have any covering overhead and nothing along the sides to protect them from the outside elements.

"Fair warning," Kamran said to their group. "Use the bathroom *before* we leave the hotel. Trust me on that."

Only a few took him up on that directive, including Ellena, who had learned when Kamran said something, he wasn't making small talk.

Now they were at a storefront and two men were working on the SUVs.

"What are they doing?"

"Taking the air out of the tires," Kamran answered.

"Why?"

"Because we cannot ride the sand on full ones."

"You're saying all of us are going into the Sand dunes in luxury SUVs?"

"That is about the size of it," Kamran said, glancing down at her.

"But wouldn't Jeeps be a better way to go?"

"Not if you want to be comfortable." Kamran leaned against the truck. "I did not want that kind of experience for you. You will have to trust me on that."

"I have to use the bathroom," Patrice squeaked.

Kamran sighed, and placed a hand on his forehead. "Did I not tell you to—"

"Yes, but my kidneys are screaming something different," Patrice snapped, shrugging. "That cough and sneeze hits different after forty. So, like I said, I have to go."

He gestured past the throng of aggressive salesmen touting head coverings and other items people might need for the trip. Kamran and Ellena's group were already properly prepared. That other group, not so much. Those salesmen made a killing off them.

Several minutes later, Patrice and a few others returned, clearly shaken by their experience. He tossed them some hand sanitizers and held up his hands for them not to come any closer. "Use that first, thank you."

Patrice used damn near the whole bottle.

Dolly and Damaris turned toward each other, clearly trying not to burst out laughing.

"Kamran, why didn't you tell us that they didn't have a real bathroom?" Patrice screeched. "That was literally a hole in the ground!" She shuddered and looked ready to pass out.

"I did warn you," he said, trying to hold back a laugh.

Ellena looked at him until he fell silent, then he burst out laughing at the same time Dolly and Damaris did. "The oasis has portable ones," he said after he regained his composure. "But here, not so much. Dolly and Damaris, cut it out," he warned, trying not to laugh again—and failing. "You all are such a bad influence."

"I've heard of hole in the walls, but hole in the ground?" Patrice griped as Dolly fell into Damaris' arms, bodies shaking so hard because they could not contain their humor.

"And if anyone has a heart condition or back troubles, you will not wish to take this route," he said to the group. "Two of the trucks will take the road that leads to the oasis. You will want to be in one of those."

"How do you know where to go?" Ellena asked, scanning the area with mountains of sand that stretched in every direction as far as the eye could see.

"The GPS is set to an actual range of geographic coordinates," Kamran answered, opening the door for her and the rest of the women riding with them. "And there is a lead car who keeps everyone on point."

Kamran started slow, getting them accustomed to the ebb and flow of ambling up sand mountains, then angling on the side to make it to a lower level point. The feel was that of a roller coaster, as each uphill climb was steep. Screams and squeals of terror reigned supreme and echoed in the SUV. Kamran's intense concentration remained on handling the vehicle through the undulating terrain.

"Has anyone ever—"

Kamran's eyebrows shot up, but he did not take his eyes off the sand.

"You know."

"Yes," he admitted, catching on to the fact that Ellena didn't want to frighten anyone by voicing her concern out loud. "Those who do not take this seriously."

"All right," she whispered and put a tighter grip on that "hold onto your ass" bar above the passenger window. "Soooo, how much more of this?"

"Twenty minutes."

"All right."

Kamran sighed as he grimaced. "Did I not warn you that—"

"Yes, yes you did. But you didn't say we could lose our lives."

"And I am going slow," he protested, angling the SUV up another steep climb. "If I had my nephew Kamal, with me, he would be asking me what the hell is wrong with me."

"Did you say lose a life?" Dolly asked in a breathy whisper.

Kamran briefly looked at her in the rearview mirror. "She's being dramatic."

"No, I'm not," Ellena protested. "This whole man against machine against nature thing is giving me—"

"Mr. Kamran."

"Yes, Sheree."

"I have a heart murmur," she whined, placing a hand over her chest. "I can't take any more of this."

His head whipped up and he slowed the vehicle to a halt. "You are serious?" He sighed, closed his eyes for a second as his lips twitched. "Did I not—"

"Yes, yes, yes. I know you did," she cried and her voice wavered. "And I'm so sorry. But please get me out of here. Please, please."

Kamran closed his eyes for a moment, then called the lead driver to let him know of the new developments. Shortly after, another SUV, an empty one, pulled to the top of a sand hill. Kamran left the driver's side, opened the back door and asked, "Do the rest of you wish to go forward or want to go back?"

Dolly and Damaris said, "We'd like to finish the trip."

"Kamran?" Ellena hedged.

"Stay put, I will be right back."

He gently guided the more adventurous of his current group on the trek up the hill and situated them into another SUV.

Sheree watched the entire exchange and said a tearful, "I'm sorry."

"I'm not," Ellena shot back. "I don't have a heart condition, but the fear that this truck could tip over is real."

"He looked so upset."

"No, just irritated," Ellena said, trying to reassure the petite red-haired woman. "I think he likes driving these."

Kamran slid back into the driver's seat and said, "Now, I will go very slow until we make it to the entrance, all right? We will have to go back the way we came, though, there is no getting around that. We are in the middle of the sand dune and there is no other way."

"How long to our destination?" Ellena asked.

"Sixteen minutes ahead. Thirteen to go back."

Ellena addressed her classmate. "Three minutes, Sheree?"

"I want to go back," she squeaked, putting a grip on the leather seats. "I swear it felt like I was dying."

"How often do you get to drive the dunes?" Ellena asked as Kamran slowly inched the SUV in the opposite direction.

"Rarely. As Royal Advisor, it is not a pleasure I can indulge in often."

"I'm sorry, Kamran."

He looked at Sheree in the rear view mirror, his voice was patient and kind as he said, "It is fine, do not worry."

Unfortunately, in the long drive around, they hit a major traffic snarl, and they missed the camel rides, some of the entertainment, and getting henna tattoos. They were only able to snag a plate of food because their group was situated in the VIP area with special, more comfortable seating.

"I'm so sorry," Sheree said.

"No worries," Kamran said, then whispered to Ellena, "I will make this up to you some other time."

Chapter 10

"I have shown you most of the sites that Durabia has to offer," Kamran said on the evening of day eight, taking a seat across from her at the dining room table of the suite. "Now I must give you more of the truth, yes?"

The guards and assistants had already retired to their accommodations down the hall.

Ellena laid her fork on the edge of the plate, sobered by his ominous tone. She pondered his words for a moment. The last few days, the group had experienced a river boat cruise, a visit to the museum, the reunion dinner where more classmates had flown in, and the magnificent Grand Mosque in Abu Dhabi, a city that was part of the United Arab Emirates. An interesting visit, one where four of her classmates failed to heed Kamran's warning and were turned back to buy clothes in the shopping center that would cover them properly. "I'm covered enough," one of them complained. "What they want us to do, die? It's hot out here." Well, they wanted to see the place and had no choice but to comply—heat and all.

"Yes, I want the truth," she answered Kamran.

"There is a public face of Durabia for tourists and a private one for Nationals."

She waved that thought away. "What do you mean? Everything you've shown me has been amazing."

"Yes, this is the side that only expatriates and tourists see," he said over the rim of his glass. "That is all that they are allowed to see. You, my love, have had the honor of a visit to the Royal Palace. Many have never set foot anywhere close to where you have been." Kamran took her hands in his. "If you made a decision based on what you have seen, your answer would be …"

"Yes. Definitely yes."

"And that would not be fair," Kamran countered. She didn't miss the uncharacteristic anxiety in his tone. "And it would be selfish of me not to give you everything to consider. Even when it might not work in my favor."

"I'm listening."

Kamran sighed, gathering his thoughts. "Are you familiar with Sharia Law? "

She filtered through her memories to every bit of news, video clips, or articles that she'd come across that referenced that term. "I've heard of it. Nothing good. Seems restrictive, especially for women. A more extreme form of Islam."

"There is some truth to your observation," he said, and his voice sounded solemn and grave. "Durabia is under Sharia Law."

Ellena laughed and it took her a minute to realize he was dead serious. "No, not possible. Women were walking around without head coverings and some even had short dresses. Not too short, but still their shoulders and arms were bare. People drink spirits and party and all of that."

"Yes, that is true," he said in measured tones. "Now, I would like you to close your eyes.

She moved her plate of East Indian delicacies aside and complied.

"Describe what you saw in the palace, in and around the palace grounds."

Her eyes were moving behind those lids as she sifted through her second day in Durabia. Her lips parted slightly and he resisted the urge to kiss her because the moment was too serious for distractions. She didn't speak, but her body became tense. Her eyes flew open and the alarm within those dark-brown orbs was not hard to miss. The Free Zone and the Royal palace were two different worlds. Now she knew why.

"You understand the point I am making?"

She nodded.

"It will be like that every day, all day. *Fully* covered, except for your face and in certain areas where having your hair exposed is allowed. Prayer, five times a day whether you are a believer or not. Separate facilities for women and men and—"

"There's more?"

"Because you are …" He grimaced, trying to find politically correct terms.

"What?"

"American. Not a national. You may experience some … mistreatment, even. Verbally. Perhaps, physically. Punishments are absolute."

She pondered that for several moments and let her gaze travel around the room then settle on him. "Could I live in unrestricted Durabia? The Free Zone?"

Kamran's shoulders pulled back. "You desire to become my wife?"

"I would be honored."

The relief that flooded his being was pure magic. A lot had transpired in his life and his path was set in a predictable journey. Having Ellena in his life would make for exciting times. "I will talk to my father and see about a residence in the Free Zone. Are you sure?"

"I'm sure," she said as he took her hands into his across the table.

"You still will be held to the constraints of Sharia Law."

"Even though I'm not Muslim?"

"Yes," he admitted. "You are still aligned with the Royal Family and will be held to the standards of conducting your person." He went silent and his heart sank. "Since we have been together, I have never witnessed you in prayer or seen any outward sign that you believe in God."

"My God does not require an outward show of anything," she countered. "The relationship is personal and one on one."

"You are completely Christian, yes?"

She hesitated a moment. "I can't claim that so much either. It's hard to believe in a God that would allow so much evil to permeate this world. And I realize that our true religion and culture was taken and a new one was forced upon us, but that isn't the reason I haven't embraced the religion. I do think that God knows exactly what and who we mean when we worship, even if the medium might be different."

Some of her words were disheartening to hear. He thought for sure that this aspect would be something that might be navigated with a bit of finesse, but having her shut things down completely blew that idea out of the water. His gaze came back to her from the view of the river when she spoke again.

"But even though I don't wholeheartedly embrace Christianity, I can't see myself embracing Islam, either. At the core, the treatment of Black people and women is about the same."

"It is no different than American men, who treat their women—as possessions."

"Not all men do, and it isn't the law. How would Islam be better?" she shot back. "If I'm going to put myself into a situation like that, at least there should be some advantages."

"How about if that situation came with a husband like me?" He wiggled his eyebrows.

"Well there is that," she said, smiling for the first time in the last moments. "I won't lie to you. I'm falling for you hard—but I can't stay here if it requires converting. Someone like me would constantly be in harm's way and feel threatened under this kind of restrictive laws," she confessed. "I'm afraid."

"I will not lie to you either. So am I."

"Why are you afraid?" she asked, narrowing her eyes on him. "You have everything."

Kamran locked a heated gaze on her. "I do not have you."

Chapter 11

Ellena's heart constricted when Kamran bid her farewell, then escorted her from the dining room table to the door to the master bedroom.

"Stay with me," she whispered, looking up at him, her heart pounding a river of heated blood through her veins. As much as she tried to talk herself into forgoing her way of life to be with him, fear shut those thoughts down. "This one last night, stay with me."

Kamran lowered to the bed by her side, he stroked her face with his fingertips. "I cannot do that. It is hard enough to say farewell and send you on your way. But to know that it is my religion that separates us is a bitter pill to swallow. And there is nothing I can do, nothing at all."

"It is not the religion; it is the *interpretation* of it that can get me killed, Kamran." She cupped his face in her hands. "I don't know how it happened. I don't know when it happened. But this place right here"—she placed his hand over her heart—"hasn't felt anything for anyone in a very long time. And it never was this strong. Ever. I'm already missing you and I'm not even gone. Please stay with me until tomorrow."

"I cannot, and—"

"Why?"

Kamran ran a hand through his hair, exhaling his frustration. "Woman, I have needs. Strong ones. And they have been dormant for a long while." His gaze was so intense she thought she would melt right then and there. "I want to be inside you so badly that I ache, beloved. But I am afraid if I have one taste, one touch, it will not be enough. And I want to be good about keeping my promise to let you go." He lowered his gaze to their hands. "I understand your decision. I do not like it, but I understand and I would not have you do anything that puts such fear in your heart. My kingdom is not going to change any time soon. No matter what I would prefer."

She simply looked at him and in her eyes he saw such sadness. This truly affected her more than he believed possible.

"Please, my love," he said, kissing her temple. "I need to sleep alone tonight in the other bedroom. I need to reflect on why Allah would give me such a beautiful gift, then take it in the next breath. Another cruelness played upon my life."

Kamran released her and swept from the room leaving an echo of sadness in his wake.

A tear came and then another, but all thought of giving in and staying in the palace of Durabia faded when voices inside the suite signaled that he wasn't simply going to the other bedroom. He was leaving her ... for good.

"Kamran, where are you going?" she asked, rushing to the foyer.

"I will see you in the morning," he said, from his place near the doorway. "At the palace. This is best."

She nodded, unable to speak her piece. She couldn't trust her voice to say anything that mattered. Her heart was breaking when she hadn't realized it could be filled enough to break. Kamran had. In nine days, this man had done exactly what he said he would do—make her fall in love with him. The best parts of him. The sincere parts of him.

So much so, that he loved her enough to be honest and give her the choice, when he could have easily allowed things to move forward and she would have had to deal with this part of things after it was too late. He loved her enough to let her go. He loved her enough to know that if they made love even just one time, that he wouldn't be able to keep his promise because she would become his and he would fight like hell to keep her with him.

"Rashid, give us a minute, please."

He looked to Kamran who said, "I will be out shortly."

Ellena's mind filtered through a range of scenarios. She did not want to lose him, but she also did not care to become a stranger in a faraway land. "You are able to come to the States from time to time?"

Kamran placed his back against the door. "No."

"So, if I leave my information you can't come to me in America?"

"No," he said, gaze narrowed as realization dawned. "I am the Royal Advisor to the ruling Sheikh of Durabia. I am not allowed to leave Durabia at any time. The punishment for doing so would be harsh."

"Then we have no choice," she said in breathy voice. She slid off the tunic, leaving only a silky undergarment in place. She lowered the strap until one nipple was exposed.

Kamran tore his gaze away, released a steady stream of breaths before a string of what she perceived as curses in Arabic left his lips. "Ellena, do not do this," he pleaded. "Not until you are my wife. And if you are not staying …"

She moved forward. "Do you know the words that will join us in matrimony?"

"Yes."

"Then Allah will know what's in your heart and mine. The Sheikh already sanctioned our marriage. This will be one that is ours, not anyone else's. Speak the words. Now."

He tilted his head, peered at her a moment, then said the words in Arabic, had her repeat the necessary ones. Then she moved towards him.

"Under the eyes of God, under the eyes of the laws of Durabia, I, Ellena Marie Kiley, accept Kamran Ali Khan as my husband," she said in a sure, strong voice.

"And I, Kamran Ali Khan of the House of Maharaj, accept you, Ellena Marie Kiley, as my wife."

Ellena was in his arms, and he held her so close she thought she would shatter under the weight of his need. Then she looked up at him and Kamran gave her a small smile. "For now, we have no choice but to join this way," she said. "With a woman who is willing to be yours completely. And a man who has demonstrated his love just by being who he is. If this one night is all we have … then let's make it last forever."

Kamran scooped her off her feet, carried her to the draped, king-size bed and unveiled the other breast, drawing one bud between his lips. Teasing, tasting her before trailing his lips up the smooth curve of her shoulder, to the graceful lines of her neck, then following to the point of her chin that elicited a tiny laugh because of her sensitivity. Then he claimed her mouth, pressing one kiss, then another and yet another in quick succession, before parting her lips to heatedly explore the moist depths.

She trembled beneath him, her thighs parted before gripping his outer thighs. She palmed his buttocks, pulling him close.

Kamran gave a low, throaty chuckle. "Patience, my love. Patience."

The kiss deepened and her hold on him tightened as his hands stroked her body, first playing in those tiny locs before creating a heated path all the way to her belly, thighs, then feet, igniting a flame as though impressing every inch of her to memory.

"Kamran ..."

"Patience."

Every touch was torture as he positioned between her thighs. This one night might be all they had for a long while. He planned to drink every drop of his delicious fill.

At that moment she pleaded with him again, only then did he part her core and slowly entered that welcoming heat. The heavy warmth of arousal signaled the need to release his seed deep within. He shivered with the effort it took not to plunge into her with no regard for her pleasure. In a second, he remembered that doing so would bear no fruit. For an instant, regret filled him, for the children they would not have. For not having the pleasure of seeing their likeness or lifelines extended.

If Allah granted him another blessing, besides keeping Ellena in his life, having a child would be the one he desired.

"Kamran..."

"Yes, my love."

"I need you to quit playing and do the damn thing."

"But I thought foreplay was ..." Kamran's eyebrow shot up.

"Make love now," she commanded. "Foreplay later."

He locked gazes with Ellena. Her expression was both a challenge and a dare. With one thrust he was in deep, so deep, a growl—primitive and powerful—came with it. Another prayer for his seed to stay put, allowing him to enjoy the moist heat of her. He strained with the effort and willed himself not to release. She reached down between them and made a ring of her fingers. Then she pressed at the base of his shaft and the need to release subsided.

Kamran looked down at her. Her hips moved, and all thoughts escaped his mind. He joined her rhythm, extracting himself only to plunge into her again and again, then he halted.

"Kamran…"

"Ellena."

A kiss again joined them above as well as below. She pressed at his base once more, keeping his release at bay.

"My God," he whispered against her hair. "You are exquisite."

"You're not so bad yourself."

Minutes later, he reached the pinnacle of no return. From deep within, his seed burst forth in hard jet streams that shook his entire being. He held on to Ellena to anchor himself and keep him tethered to this world.

Chapter 12

"Did you just call on Christ?" she asked, several minutes later.

Kamran inhaled, still reeling from his first intimate encounter in years. He glanced at her, smiling between breaths. "It was the best sensual experience I have ever had. But I am not changing religions."

Ellena winced, then threw her head back and laughed. The sound lightened his soul.

"And, yes, I did see *Harlem Nights*. And I swear I saw the light, and you might have almost sent me to meet my Maker, but I promise you I did not call on the Christ to help me through that most amazing experience."

"Then I must not have been doing something right." Ellena repositioned herself until she straddled his thighs, guiding him into her heat once again. "Let me give it another try."

Kamran gripped her hips as she rotated on him with torturous, slow motions. Then they quickened, and so did his breathing.

Minutes ticked by, the pulse of heat at the base of his erection signaled another orgasm was eminent. His head reared back, a growl erupted before a sharp intake of breath. The exquisite sensations elicited a roar of pleasure that emerged as a bellow of blended pain and joy.

Moments later, Rashid and Waqas were banging on the door to the suite. Kamran's cell lit up with a flurry of texts and calls.

"I believe they think you are in here causing my demise."

"Well, you need to go tell them something."

He swung his legs over to the side and froze. "I am not going to the door like this," he protested. "I can barely feel my legs."

More banging.

"So, you want me to stroll out there and let them see me all love-swept and disheveled." She placed her hand on her forehead for dramatic affect.

"You are such an actress."

Kamran wasn't all the way out of the bed before Rashid and Waqas rushed in, eagle-eyed gazes sweeping the area.

"Halt," Kamran commanded before they made it past the dining room.

"Sir, I … Oh …" Rashid stood ramrod straight. "Sir, please forgive me."

Waqas quickly averted his gaze.

"You don't know what screams of passion sound like?"

Rashid stiffened under the weight of that query. "First of all, it was not a scream, sir. Second, yes I know what mine sounds like but in the years I have worked for you, I have never known what *yours* sound like."

"You could not think that Ellena was harming me."

"It is our business to make sure nothing untoward is happening in this suite," Rashid said, trying to form a scowl. "You are still an unmarried man."

"Was that Dolly *and* Damaris I saw tip back into your suite earlier?" Kamran leaned in to whisper to them, quirking an eyebrow as Rashid's complexion flushed with color.

Waqas whispered, "My apologies, I—"

"Good night, Waqas. Rashid."

"Yes sir," Rashid said in a defeated voice. "We will stay right outside."

Ellena's laughter floating from the bedroom caused their faces to redden.

Chapter 13

"Does she taste like chicken?" Amir taunted, adjusting his head covering.

Laraib, Kamran's next oldest brother, held his belly to contain himself as he said, "Maybe watermelon, yes?"

Those vicious words from his brothers brought a range of laughter, guffaws, and chuckles from the men in the foyer of the throne room. Uncles, brothers, and cousins all found humor at Ellena's expense.

Kamran smiled at Amir and Laraib, who stood next to Nadeem one minute, then they were trying to pick themselves up from the marble flooring the next minute, while the men nearby gaped. The elegance of the cream walls and cushioned seating were at odds with the murmur of disapproval that erupted.

"Tah-hathek! You struck me?" Amir bellowed, trying to keep in a loose front tooth with one hand. His statement meant, may all of your luck be taken away. When he was the one who needed it right now because Kamran was ready to tell him "Tozz Feek"—*screw you* and the camel you rode in on.

"Just wondering," Kamran said, glaring down at the man. "Did that taste like victory or did it taste like defeat?"

Umar, Kamran's younger brother, moved in to help Laraib from the marble tiles.

"You would strike them over a woman?" Uncle Sufian bellowed.

"Yes, I would," Kamran confirmed, squaring his shoulders. "But he had better be glad I did not kill him for an insult to my wife. That is a lesson everyone in this room will need to learn."

"You are not married yet," Salman said through his teeth. Yet another brother who was the spitting image of their father.

"Father sanctioned it and in the eyes of Allah, we are. I would love for you to test me on that score."

The silence that met that threat was almost an entity unto itself.

Kamran stepped away from Amir, who still couldn't manage to stay upright.

"I cannot control what is said when I am not around, but in my presence, if you even *think* about slighting Ellena in anyway, I will give you plenty to think about and even more to recover from."

"She is not even a national," his brother, Nadeem, snarled. "You did not even know her nine sunsets ago. Where is this coming from? She has no value."

"She has no value to you," he tossed back, closing the distance between them and causing his brother to retrace his steps to a safer place. "Neither does your own wife. What other reason do you have to portray a loving, doting husband within these walls, then grace the confines of El Zalaam outside and mate with girls who cannot even be presented in a legal marriage here?"

Nadeem averted his gaze to some of the other men in the room.

Ones who also indulged in the wicked, and often illegal pleasures that El Zalaam had to offer.

"You know we do not speak of these things," Umar warned, then he straightened to his full height, which was still six inches less than Kamran. "We are entitled to fleshly pleasures that will fulfill us. What good is having wealth if we are not able to indulge?"

"Yes, it is written somewhere, defile yourself with a child and enter into the gates of heaven. I would love for you to show me where that is in the Qur'an."

Salman ignored that slight and peered at Amir. "How bad is it?"

"I think two loose teeth," Amir answered, his voice muffled by the effort to speak normally.

"A broken nose, maybe?" Laraib replied, dabbing his nose with a tissue that Salman snagged from one of the servants.

"You will pay for this," Amir threatened. "And that Black wh—"

Kamran's eyebrow shot up and both hands balled into fists at his side. His stance caused Amir to quickly amend his words to say, "Woman, too."

"I have heard there was something called Black girl magic," Umar said as he passed Kamran on the way to the entrance. "Perhaps she has bewitched you in some way."

Salman shook his head. "Or maybe since it is his first time with a woman after all these years ..."

"See, Kamran, you should have come with us to El Zalaam. Maybe then you would not be so tightly wound about a who—woman," Salman also corrected, knowing that saying anything else would land him in the same position as the first two. "Who has no bearing on this family."

"And maybe if you all felt the same way about your wives as I do about mine, there would be enough respect to go around and no need for you to frequent places of ill repute."

"She is not even your wife," Nadeem spat.

Kamran's mind filtered through the pleasures of last night all the way to morning and said, "She is, to me. And that is all that matters." Kamran sauntered to the gold doors. "Remember what I said, and we will not have this discussion again."

He stepped over the threshold and moved from the foyer and into the throne room and an uncertain future. One where he would not be with the woman he had come to love.

Chapter 14

"Nine days, yes?" Sheikh Aayan said from his place on a golden throne. "And from what I hear you are going home?"

Ellena's gaze flickered to Kamran as she sighed. "Unfortunately, yes."

"It is a sad thing," Sheikh said, his tone solemn. "My son seems so smitten by you."

"And I, him."

The Sheikh scanned the expectant faces of those situated around the room—wives, daughters, sons, brothers, and children over the ages of twelve. "Then why are you leaving?"

"He sent word to me before I arrived that he asked you if we would be allowed to remain in the Free Zone and live there. We were denied."

The Sheikh's expression turned dark. He was obviously insulted that someone would not desire to live in the most beautiful place in the land. "So, you are leaving because you do not wish to live in the palace? Are your living accommodations so much better than ours?"

That question brought snickers and laughter from among the men in his family.

Ellena stiffened and her chin went up, but she flashed a glance at Kamran, who willed her not to say anything that would prick his father's pride, even if he deserved such a thing.

"I have no wish to embarrass my beloved because I am not used to certain situations and customs." She placed a hand over her heart. "If I say the wrong thing, it affects him. If I do the wrong thing, it affects him. I do not wish for him to be burdened with my ignorance and my fears."

The Sheikh considered her words for a moment. "Do you ... love him?"

Ellena eyed Kamran and smiled. "I did not think it possible, but yes, I do." She put her focus back to the King. "He is such a pure soul and has such integrity."

One corner of his mouth curved in a grin. "And not bad on the eyes, eh?"

A few peals of laughter and chuckles ensued.

"Really? I didn't notice it," she teased with a sly smile and a shrug.

The Sheikh raised his hand. All sounds subsided. "I am truly sorry that you are not willing to stay. But he is a Royal advisor and must remain on palace grounds, unless I am traveling elsewhere."

She nodded, then shared a glance with Kamran who winked. "I understand."

"The guards will escort you to the airport to join your friends."

Ellena made a slight bow. "Thank you for your kindness."

She gave Kamran a lingering look. He stared at her until she had no choice but to follow the guards.

"Please give this to Kamran," Ellena said, embracing Saba, who nodded and wiped away tears before accepting the slip of paper from

Ellena. The woman had been such a blessing in the days Ellena had been in Durabia and it was obvious she was rooting for something that would not happen.

"Yes, Ms. Ellena," she whispered. "Right away."

Ellena fell in step with the two men who flanked her. She glanced over her shoulder to the three men surrounding Kamran and gave Rashid, Saqab, and Waqas a nod of silent farewell. They gave her a slight bow and nod in return—even their eyes were sad.

Midway on the path to Kamran, Sheikh Khan commanded Saba, "Bring that here."

Ellena whipped around, protesting, "That is a private note for Kamran's eyes only."

"Nothing is private in my sheikhdom," he countered, leveling a gaze on Saba. "Bring it to me."

Saba's eyes widened as she shot a wary glance at Ellena, but had no choice but to do as she had been commanded.

Sheikh Aayan tore open the envelope and scanned the card. "This is a wedding invitation." He blinked twice, scowling as he scanned it once more. "Your own wedding invitation for a marriage between you and my son in the … United States?" His voice was almost a roar. "You would entice my son to permanently leave Durabia and live in America?"

"No, Sheikh," she replied. "The plan would be for him to find a way to *visit* America as often as you would allow to be with his wife. And I will visit Durabia as often as he can bring me here for me to be with my husband." She spread her hands in humble supplication. "You gave me a precious gift. I am not refusing this gift. Not at all. Since, I am not able to remain here, I'm merely finding a different place to open it. Surely, you can't fault me for that?"

Sheikh focused on the invite for several moments, then looked at her, then threw back his head and laughed. The tension in the room eased with his mirth.

"And you know I would not allow such a thing," the Sheikh said in a tight voice, then focused in on his son's face. "You would … you would defy my wishes to accept such an invitation without approval, my son?"

"Most definitely," Kamran confirmed, leveling a steely gaze on his father. "In my heart and in the eyes of Allah, she is already my wife. I was your gift to her. She is Allah's blessing to me. I do not take that lightly. And I do not take her invitation lightly, either. Neither should you."

Grumbles of discontent rumbled throughout the court, mostly from his brothers and uncles.

"Silence." Sheikh looked at the card a final time, then flickered a gaze between Ellena and Kamran several times, and it seemed an eternity before he smiled. "Well, it seems that I am an excellent matchmaker, but the law is as it is written."

Kamran's mother glided past her daughters, sister-wives. and daughters-in-law all lined opposite of the men, and asked, "May I speak?"

The Sheikh gestured for her to go on.

"The law is as you decree," she said with a humble bow. "Would it be such a disservice to allow this woman who pleases our son to remain in the Free Zone? Or a residence directly outside of the palace? Give her time to learn the customs and understand the reasons for them. Then we would address this question of residence in say five, maybe ten years?"

All kinds of relief flooded Kamran's body. His mother was pure genius. A wonderful compromise, if his father would see it in that light.

"Question, Ellena Kiley."

The Sheikh's booming voice commanded a response.

Ellena settled her attention on him.

"The only thing that stands between remaining here with my son or going home to America is your unwillingness to live in the palace with him?"

She picked apart the traps in such a loaded question, filtering through an answer that would not be an insult. "If I may be so bold," she said in measured tones as she retraced her steps to be closer to the throne. "It is not an unwillingness to live with him. It is my wish that I do not live under a law I do not understand and wasn't raised to embrace."

The Sheikh shot a glance at Kamran who wore a stoic expression, taking it all in. "Fair enough."

Ellena turned to walk away, but the guards still faced the Sheikh, waiting. She had no other choice but to turn and eyeball the Sheikh again.

"You have laws and requirements in your land?"

"Yes, sir," she answered. Kamran's nod of approval was almost imperceptible, so she continued, "And I understand them because I grew up with them. Here, not having my hair covered could land me in a world of trouble."

"So, you love him, then you cover your head and your body," Sheikh snapped, impatience coloring his tone and his expression. "That is not so hard."

"But *why* am I doing it?"

A flutter of movement and then dead silence met her question.

"Nothing's been wrong with my hair all this time. Why is it so offensive here? Why is having my arms and shoulders exposed such a sin? Is it that men are so unable to control their desires that we pay the cost for that? And what is it truly to protect me from? Rape still occurs in Islamic cultures, regardless of what clothes a woman wears. Covering doesn't keep that from happening. Seems like the problem isn't the women. So penalize the men, not us."

Sheikh Aayan's eyes widened and a vein throbbed at his temple. Kamran inhaled and tried not to smile. His woman, oh yes, his woman would question everything he believed in.

"Remember, these are part of your culture," Ellena continued. "It is part of your religion, not mine."

"People embrace new religions all the time," Sheikh Aayan said, glaring at Kamran as though he was the one challenging him in such a manner. "And especially if they love their husbands as they claim."

"That is true, but I would not embrace *this* religion," she confessed. "The disparity in the treatment of women outweighs what I'm already experiencing in America." Ellena spread her hands. "Why would I trade a religion I'm familiar with, for one that is so much more restrictive, and dangerous for me if I make a mistake? At least I understand the unfairness of American religions and laws. Here, I would be at a severe disadvantage. As much as I love your son, the risk outweighs the benefits. The fear alone is crippling. And he loves me enough that he would rather see me leave, than for me to live here with him, in fear. That is true love right there."

The Sheikh's silence caused her to chance a gaze in Kamran's direction. His slight smile was all the encouragement she needed. "Love can only carry us so far, Sheikh. When his wife is left out of a great many things because she makes simple mistakes she is unaware of, that becomes *his* shame. And he has suffered enough of that from the moment you decided he was not the son who was to sit on the throne simply because nature and genetics had other plans. That, in itself, was one cruelty compounded by another. Do not subject him to further anguish by giving him a wife who would be a constant source of embarrassment."

Kamran stiffened. So did many others.

Sheikh Aayan's face darkened with rage.

Kamran stepped forward. "Father, I—"

"You dare to judge me for a decision I made in the best interest of the kingdom," the Sheikh roared.

"No, your highness," she said in a milder tone. "I'm merely pointing out that a beloved son as you claim that he is, could have easily kept his title and position in your royal line and chosen a nephew of that same bloodline as his heir." She seemed to deliberately ignore Kamran's silent directive to pipe down. "With the action you have taken, a man who has a deep love for his people and his culture, who also has amazing ideas of how to bring even more wealth into Durabia, has been placed on the sidelines. His wisdom, knowledge and compassion for all people will die with him and not bear fruit."

She lifted her chin, meeting the Sheikh's hard glare head on. "That is a sad thing for everyone involved. Especially, when you have shown the foresight to make Durabia a place that everyone wants to experience and now call the City of the World. A metropolis. But I have seen no other initiatives and plans from any of your other sons that will enhance the splendor and economy of what you've already put in place."

A string of Arabic curses went up from one of Kamran's brothers. Another held him back when he lunged toward Ellena.

"Kamran has every aspiration of doing so," Ellena continued. "And he has the intelligence, determination, and passion needed to carry out projects far beyond even things you have planned. I have seen no such thing from any of your other sons. They seem complacent to let you do all of the work and planning, while they reap the benefits of your foresight. Kamran has no such inclination. He's a visionary, like you. He is passionate about his family, his people, and Durabia. Exactly in that order."

The silence beyond that statement was frightening.

Kamran widened his eyes, grimacing at her, sending a message, a warning to take things no further. Ellena had overstepped a boundary, even in her truth. A woman—an American—a Black woman—did not say these things to a ruling Sheikh. But oh, was his wife nailing every issue to the wall. She was nothing short of brilliant. And she was his. Every feisty ounce of her.

His father had six wives, children from each, but Salman, Amir, Laraib, Nadeem, and Umar, were now the favorites because they were the eldest sons from each wife. At one time, Kamran was the Crown Prince and none of them factored in, because he was destined to rule. Then ... he wasn't. Now five sons were jockeying for the position of Crown Prince as one act or another could take them out of consideration. Father kept them all on notice and that meant each of them did whatever it took to curry his favor. Some of their methods had been underhanded and their father did not discourage the unhealthy competition.

Kamran's position as royal advisor could be easily filled by someone else. Nothing existed for him here except his mother. He had always felt like an outsider since the day his father took away his title of Crown Prince. He had enough tucked away in Swiss accounts to carry him and his beloved in luxury for the rest of their lives. The moment Ellena was on a plane to America, he was going to find some way to be right behind her. Then if he could have his mother to follow, he didn't care if he ever came back to Durabia. He would be with his woman, whatever soil would take them both.

Ellena lowered her gaze as well as her tone. "Please forgive me, Sheikh Aayan, if I have spoken too harshly or if it was not my place to say these things. My love for Kamran is speaking and not the intelligence that says that I, a woman, should not address things as such, no matter how true they are."

The Sheikh was silent so long after her apology of sorts, Kamran thought his father did not have words to express his anger in a way that would not make him seem petulant.

"You did not like my choice of words," she said in a milder tone. "You are offended and that was not my intent. You are very much aware how Americans and Blacks are seen in your culture and religion, the same as people of color are seen in America—inferior. I do not wish for Kamran to constantly be on the defensive or have to always apologize for something that cannot be changed."

The silence was so profound, Kamran believed everyone could hear his heart slam against the wall of his chest.

"You really love him?" the Sheikh said in a tone that spoke to such a thing being an impossibility.

"Yes, and you seem surprised that I came to care for him in so little time. He is your son, yes? With all of your charm, good looks, and charisma, yes?" she challenged. "But the bigger question is why wouldn't I love him? He has a pure soul, a heart and love for his family and his culture that is so expansive, it takes my breath away."

Kamran's heart swelled with love, pride and passion. No one had ever stood up to his father on his behalf. Well, except his mother. But this woman, this *amazing* woman was fearless in voicing so many obvious things that his father tended to brush over. No, he wasn't going to be on the plane right after her, he was taking that flight out with her.

His father and his position could be damned.

Chapter 15

Sheikh Aayan waggled a finger in Ellena's direction. "She is most excellent with words. You have given me much to ponder." His gaze swept to Kamran. "And she has made an excellent case on your behalf. I would love to hear such plans that you have in mind for Durabia, my son."

Kamran nodded, but didn't miss that five of his brothers were in hushed, but heated conversations and their wives were glaring daggers at his beloved.

"Ellena," Sheikh said in a tone that made all voices trickle into silence. "I will allow you to reside in the Free Zone and remain here in Durabia as Kamran's wife."

Several shocked gasps and murmurs echoed behind that pronouncement.

"But you must attend dinner at the palace every Friday after prayer. Is that acceptable?"

Ellena looked to Kamran, who nodded vigorously.

The Sheikh noticed the exchange and smiled. "See? Already accepting your husband's wisdom. Not such a bad thing, eh?"

"And he accepts mine," she said with a lift of her chin. "It is not a one-sided thing. Balance. You listened to your own wife, yes? It is how any marriage best succeeds."

Sheikh peered at her a moment, lips twitching with the need to smile. "My son, she is a feisty one. Are you certain this is how you wish to proceed?"

"Yes father," Kamran said, willing his heart to stop pounding a river of blood to his brain. "Most definitely."

The Sheikh turned to Ellena. "And you, are these terms acceptable?"

"Yes, Sheikh."

"And the dinner requirement. You can abide by that yes?"

"Oh, yes."

"Find your place," he said, smiling down at Kamran. "Take her as your wife, my son. We will have a magnificent wedding. Ellena, you have family who will come?"

"Two sisters, a niece and nephew, and that's about it."

"So be it."

Kamran rushed toward Ellena and gathered her in his arms. Neither one of them witnessed Amir and Faiza share a speaking glance across the room.

* * *

"Kamran, I would like a private audience with you after dinner," Sheikh Aayan said.

"Yes, Father."

"Father, as Crown Prince," Amir said, moving away from his

brothers until he was a few feet from Kamran. "I should be in on the meeting as well. I, too, would like to hear such plans as something I would implement or continue when I am King."

Sheikh tilted his head, peering at him for a long moment. "How presumptuous of you. I said private meeting and that is what it will be."

Amir gave a small bow. "My apologies, Father. I only wanted to be of service."

"Be honest, you were just being nosy, brother," Kamran shot back.

Amir's lips twitched. "That, too."

Everyone retired to the dining room. Three identical tables that seated twenty-four people each had been dressed in opulent golds and creams.

"As an honor to our guest, my soon-to-be daughter-in-law, I will give her the opportunity to say the blessing over our meal. You do say blessing in America, yes?"

"Given the fact that we don't always know the origins of what's on our plates, or how angry we've made the cook, blessings are always in order."

Laughter and a few chuckles ensued.

He gestured for her to proceed. Some of the women shared a speaking glance.

"Mother-Father God," Ellena said, lowering her head. "We come humbly before you, thanking you for abundance of love, joy, peace, and mercy. For every family represented here to be under grace and bounty. We ask that you guide every thought toward compassion, understanding, and love. That you go before them, protecting them from hurt, harm, and danger. Grace every union with balance and joy. And I ask your forgiveness as I attempt to say a prayer that everyone under the sound of my voice can embrace."

Kamran nearly slid out of his chair when Ellena let loose with the Muslim prayer—in complete Arabic. Every syllable was correct. Every nuance was perfect. Her voice was magnificent and breathy, and shamefully, he felt a stir of both love and arousal on hearing the Arabic words fall from her lips.

She ended the prayer, and no one moved for several minutes. The shocked expressions were priceless.

Kamran glanced at his father, who blinked several times in his disbelief, his mouth slightly parted for several moments before he recovered, cleared his throat, and said, "Kamran, if you were able to achieve this magnificent feat in a few days, imagine what can happen in five years."

"Father, to be honest—"

Ellena flashed a warning look his way and tilted her head.

Kamran clamped down on the rest of his confession. "Yes, father. Imagine that." He gave her a warning glare of his own and mouthed the words, "We need to talk."

Chapter 16

The door to Ellena's suite in the palace didn't close all the way before Kamran whirled on her.

She held up her hands and shrank back a little. "Kamran, I know you're upset."

"Upset," he snapped. "Woman, you made me look like a damn fool."

Her shoulders lowered in defeat. "Oh, not a *damn* fool—"

"Ellena!"

"You're right," she said, grimacing as she perched on the chaise, hold up her hands in surrender. "And I apologize."

"You know Arabic?"

She shrugged. "Very little."

"Woman, you said that prayer with complete conviction," he countered, pacing the rug stretched out before the chaise. "That is not someone who knows"—he crooked his fingers as quotes—"Very little Arabic."

"I know the greetings, the prayer, and how to say 'if the Lord wills'. That is all."

"Why the prayer?" he said, pausing long enough to lock a steely glare on her. "Why *that* prayer? And your voice ... sweet Lord, in that voice ..." He closed his eyes as though trying to center himself. "My God ..."

"Kamran, please calm down." Ellena gestured to the space beside her. "I was a member of the Nation of Islam for several years."

After a few minutes, Kamran lowered into the seat, waiting. The tension was still coiled about him.

"I raised holy hell up in that organization," she confessed. "They were happy to see me leave. For a time, I was searching for something and I sought understanding from many religions. I grew up Christian and some of the things I experienced didn't make me want to remain one. So, I went from Baptist to Methodist, then to Apostolic for one day—"

Kamran shook his head. "A religion for only one day?"

"I was in their tarry room for nearly nine hours trying to receive the gift of tongues—something they said would be a sign that I was saved and would make it into Heaven." She shrugged. "It never happened. The next Sunday I went straight to the Nation of Islam because I thought it would be better than Christianity. I found that *all* religions have their flaws and issues, especially surrounding women and in their origins and dealings with people who look like me."

Kamran absorbed that for a moment. "You said something about raising hell."

"Finally, the disparity—the difference in how women and men were treated when it came to offenses—were too much for me."

Ellena explained how women who were found to be in error or did something against the laws of the religion, they were brought before the congregation and marched out—excommunicated. But with the men, when they were found to be in sexual error, a different approach was taken. The men would not be honest. Instead, they claimed that the women were already in a relationship with them before they came into the Nation. Or they married those women very quickly to avoid any consequence. Her main issue was that the women called MGT, which stood for Military Girls Training, were keeping themselves chaste, preparing for the men—the Fruit of Islam—or FOI. Men who would never be available because they weren't keeping it together long enough to be with the women who were doing all the right things.

"The hell part?" Kamran prompted, sliding to the edge of the bench. "I am looking forward to your rebellion. You have already caused enough of a stir with my family. So this should be interesting."

Ellena continued, sharing about a team of young men whose assignment was to weed out the women who were not keeping to the laws of the Nation. Any woman who fell for their ploys to sleep with one of those team members, was excommunicated. But because the men were on "assignment," they were absolved of any wrongdoing. Though they, too, had indulged in sinful acts.

She had only figured out what was happening when Brother Nate suddenly became so aggressive with trying to get her in bed. She didn't even know how he managed to acquire her phone number. Ellena demanded that he stop calling; something that he ignored. Then when she cornered Brother Nate in the parking lot of the Mosque one day after Sunday service, she put a death grip on his groin and demanded the reason he wouldn't leave her alone. He confessed that she was on the list of women this secret group wanted out of the organization because she was running a successful event planning outfit and did not allow one of the brothers to work with her and take the lead of her business. A secret group, because the Minister would not approve of such deception. Ever.

Kamran flinched, but remained silent.

"I became angry," Ellena said, then averted her gaze, putting it squarely on the window overlooking the gardens. "I wrote a letter to the Minister, asking a question."

"That said …" Kamran hedged when Ellena averted her gaze.

"Since the MGT were doing what we were supposed to do and the FOI were doing something entirely different, could we at least masturbate since it didn't look like we were going to be married to any member of FOI any time soon."

Kamran smacked a hand to his forehead. "You did not."

She gave him a sheepish grin. "Actually, I did."

"To a high-ranking religious Muslim leader?"

Ellena shrugged, unbothered by his alarm. "I needed answers."

Kamran closed his eyes, and rubbed his forehead for a few moments before saying, "Go on."

She had been called before the MGT and FOI captains and admonished for what she had written. They didn't ask about the rest of those accusations and assertions regarding the men, or about that secret team led by Brother Nate and a few rebels running game on the women. Unfortunately, the details of that letter made the rounds through the Mosque and set tongues wagging and accusations hurling. She was invited to the Minister's lavish home in Kenwood, and had dinner with the top brass of the Nation during Ramadan—a fast that Muslims observed.

After dinner, the Minister requested a private audience, then complimented her on efforts that resulted in the creation of the Nation's junior mosque. Something that came about when her then four-year-old nephew, Christian, stated that there was nothing in the regular mosque for him. He would rather go to church because they had Sunday School for little guys like him. Then the Minister ended the conversation and basically said, "Sister Ellena, some of my best followers are *outside* of the Nation."

Kamran frowned, processing those words. "What is that supposed to mean?"

"As my niece, Blair, and nephew, Christian, both say ... deuces." Ellena gave a sideways peace sign to illustrate her point.

"You were asked to leave?"

"In so many words," she replied, smiling. "But it wasn't a bad thing. I took a lot away from my time there. Discipline and I still don't eat pork." She lowered her gaze to the hands folded on her lap. "But the prayer. I impressed myself by learning it. Sometimes I say it in reverence to God, because God knows what I mean. I'll say the Twenty-third Psalm, or a Bahá'í prayer." As her memories stirred, she closed her eyes and let her head rest against the back of the bench. "And then sometimes I draw all the way back from my childhood and I'll stand in the shower and sing *Father I Stretch My Hands to Thee*. It's a song that the Deacons or Mother's Board sang to start church services. Then I'll flow into *Guide Me Oh Thou Great Jehovah*. Those make me feel better. Whether I call God the Creator, Jehovah, Allah, The Source, The Universe—God knows exactly what I mean. He or She—as God is a spirit and has no gender, has been knowing what Black people mean for centuries. The knowledge of our true God was taken, along with our culture and knowledge of self. We didn't ask for that. But it's the respect and reverence to All That Is that matters most."

Kamran stiffened and there was a vein throbbing at his temple

"So, I never say there is only one path," she said in a soft tone. "None of the religions travels a pure road, Kamran. None of them. Except, maybe, Baha'i—since that is the *one* religion that talks peace, equality, and furthering the development of all woman and mankind, and actually means it. One that talks connection to God and humanity and actually lives up to it. If I were going to embrace a religion—it would be *that one* more than any others because it at least encompasses and respects all religions, genders, ethnic backgrounds. There's a place for me within that understanding."

Kamran gestured in a dismissive manner, scoffing as he said, "You're only feeling this way about Islam not being the religion to embrace because *that* Nation of Islam is not *pure* Islam."

"Look at you," she snapped and glared at him. "Judging them based on how the religion was brought to Black people in America. Islam, as you all worship, would have kept most of us Christian. Trust me. You think your form of Islam is better? Really?" she scoffed. "Muslims played a part in slavery, too. In some areas they still enslave African girls to this day. How *dare* you say it isn't real. You are judging the Nation's practices by *your* standards, your culture, and not by the fact that the Minister taught people who knew nothing—or never even wanted to embrace Islam—until it was presented in a way we could understand."

"I am not judging," he defended, and pulled away. But that was exactly the case. "I just think if you had a better understanding of Islam, you would see things different. That is all."

"Then let me ask you this," she snapped, and he flinched a little. "How are we supposed to embrace a religion that treats women and Blacks no better than the white Americans in power, racists, and bigots, treat us? I mean, people who forced their tainted version of Christianity on us and still expects us to embrace the forgiving and turn the other cheek part of it?"

She lasered her focus on him. "Nothing that Christ taught covered that kind of life-long chattel slavery, abuse, and downright torture. No matter how many people want to claim slavery is in all cultures, it was never to the degree of chattel slavery in America. That wasn't of Christ, but the Bible has been misused for that end. When the truth of it is that we were commodity—it was about money. The parts where slaves were to be treated fairly and, at some point, earn their freedom—like in the Bible, and every other culture—was totally overlooked."

Kamran's eyes glazed over a little and she could tell this was effecting him deeply—at it should. He couldn't consider having her as his wife, without knowing these things.

"The fact that they considered us beasts and it was a sin—according to their own Bible—to sleep with beasts, but they raped the women and children anyway—shows *exactly* how much of the Bible they believed. At least, until it suited them to ignore things." She inhaled, this was taking so much out of her, but it was ground that definitely needed to be covered. Otherwise, he would hold out hope that she would convert to a religion she couldn't embrace any more than she could totally embrace the one she grew up with.

"Only when politics came into play and the North wanted to strip the South of its power and money base that was held through slaves and what they brought to the economy, is what finally forced the slave's release. Not because of some moral or religious conviction—it was *money*. Some were born a slave and died a slave. No other slavery had that taint on it. No other type of slavery was so soul-damaging. Christ would *never* have sanctioned chattel slavery or abject greed. Not the Christ—the religion was named after."

Kamran's eyebrows drew in, absorbing her words. The silence went on for such a long time, she realized he was truly processing everything she had said. "You have taught me more about American history and the experiences of your people there. And your experience with the Nation of Islam."

The moment resignation and understanding flickered in those dark brown eyes, Ellena placed a hand over his.

"If five years is all I will have with you," he said. "Then I need to make sure it feels like an eternity in Heaven."

She lowered her gaze to hide her tears and said, "I apologize if I embarrassed you earlier."

"I was shocked." He guided her onto his lap and held onto her. "It was magnificent. But I do not wish for them to believe that I had something to do with your knowledge."

"You did," she countered. "I have never said that prayer outside of my home. In the shower mostly. Saying it tonight made me a little less of an outsider, less of an outside wife, and a little more of a wife who might fit in."

Kamran kissed her gently. "You are so wise."

"Thank you."

"And we will not inform them that you do not actually speak the language," Kamran warned.

"Why?"

"So they will be less likely to insult you within your hearing."

Ellena searched his eyes for a moment. "Will you teach me?"

"I would like nothing better." He guided her to stand, then placed another kiss to her lips. "Rest now."

"You can't stay?"

"No, my love. Not until we are properly committed to one another in the eyes of my family—and yours."

"But I promise to be good," she said in a sulky voice. "And ... And ... And, I won't ..."

Kamran gave her a parting kiss. "Sweet dreams. You have given me much to ponder. I will come for you first thing in the morning."

Chapter 17

"She is going to be a problem," Faiza said, removing her headpiece and gently placing it on the chaise. Their suite had been done in reds and creams, her favorite colors a drastic difference from the suites claimed by Kamran and Ellena—theirs were done in the Durabia royal colors.

Amir dropped his dishdasha onto the floor. "How?"

"I have a really bad feeling about all of this." Faiza nodded as she peered up at him. "Your father makes an exception for her. He allows Ellena to live in the Free Zone, but the rest of us are restricted to the palace grounds. That is so unfair." Her lips formed a pout. "I want to live in the Free Zone, too. I would like a break from all of these extensive requirements."

"She is a heathen, a nonbeliever. What does it matter?" he said with a dismissive gesture. "I do not wish to see her at family meals every day. It is fine."

Faiza gripped his arms. "No, I am telling you there is more at work here. Now your father is having private meetings with Kamran? He has never done that before. Your father is getting old, sentimental."

"I will admit that it bothered me at first," Amir said, shaking her off so he could move further into the room and discard his remaining garments. "But there is nothing that my father will keep from me."

"Is there not?"

Amir paused, retracing his steps until he stood in front of the woman many considered to be the most beautiful in the sheikhdom. "Why do you insist that one woman is going to change our way of life?"

"Because she will," she spat. "Your father would never have allowed any of you to take a nonbeliever to mate."

"Special circumstances. Kamran was never going to have a permanent mate here. He cannot sire children. And you must remember she will never rise to any status that will concern us." He shrugged. "Ellena Kiley is nothing."

Faiza closed her eyes and exhaled. "I am just grateful they will not have children," she said. "Then we will have a real problem."

Amir stared at his reflection in the floor-length mirror. "When I am king, I will banish Kamran and his heathen wife from Durabia."

"That cannot happen soon enough," she snarled. "Your father is lingering on the throne out of spite."

"No, he says I am not ready to rule."

"Pshaw!" Faiza said, placing her hands on his shoulders. "That is not the point. He, even in his advanced age, is not ready to relinquish power."

"He is the reason Durabia is the City of the World. People love him." He had tired of an argument that seemed to be ongoing.

"They need to learn to love *you*." She slapped her hands on his chest. "Have you put any plans in place that you can share with your father? Show him you are ready to move Durabia even further into progress."

He lowered his gaze to his hands. "Ellena was right about one thing. My father has done all the work," he answered with a shrug. "There is nothing for me to do but carry out his plans."

She threw up her hands and inched backward. "And that is where you err. He believes you are not ready because you do not have an initiative of your own. Trust me, Kamran does. And after such a vehement endorsement by his pet heathen, Kamran will now have his ear."

"Careful, wife," Amir warned with a level glare. "Your claws are showing."

"Claws, eh?" she snapped. "Did you hear her suggestion about the Sheikh's error in bypassing Kamran when he could have made a nephew your brother's successor instead of producing a child. That would put Kamran squarely on the throne. That one is clever, intelligent. What she states is something that I have feared all along." Faiza's expression reflected pure disdain. "She is manipulative, conniving and she is sooo ... round."

"She is curvaceous," Amir countered. "Evidently, Kamran likes that."

"She is plain," she scoffed and sat on their bed.

"She is beautiful to him. Do you see the way she lights up when he looks at her?" He stared at her for a few seconds. "They are actually in love. What are the odds?"

"How can he love a fat cow like her?" she snarled, her hazel eyes flashing with fire. "He is just elated he now has something to put his qadib into."

Amir shrugged, sliding off his sandals. "He always had a place to do that."

"But did he ever avail himself of that pleasure?"

He blinked twice, shifted on the floor as he mulled over an answer. "No."

"And your father knows it," she said with a sly smile. "Kamran holds himself to a higher standard—even higher than you."

Amir moved toward the wall adjacent to the closets, looking at her in the mirror. "What I do in the Free Zone is not your concern."

"It is your father's concern," she shot back. "He despises the fact that the men in this family indulge in such base actions as relations with girls."

"They are women," he defended.

"They are girls," she screamed, getting to her feet. "And some are there against their will. That is despicable. You have a wife. What does it say that you have me and yet seek out other women?"

Amir swept his shame aside and roared, "I have desires you cannot fulfill. I do not want the same mouth kissing my children that has been wrapped around my qadib."

Faiza flinched. "You are an animal."

"And thanks to the El Zalaam, you do not know how much of that is true."

Chapter 18

"Alejandro, I have good news and I have bad news," Ellena said to her boss, watching as Saba laid out a choice of silky garments that Kamran had sent over. The purple and golds of her suite were blended perfectly to create the ambiance of royalty, but the décor was simple and a bit muted after staying within the luxurious Jumillah.

"Give me the bad news first," Dro said, and the shuffle of papers on the other end signaled he was in the middle of analyzing something. As a "Fixer" he had been part of some behind the scenes activities—worldwide—for private companies, individuals and governments. Everything from "rescues", intel, covert operations and missions that would keep political regimes from failing.

"I won't be coming back to America."

Dro paused a long while. "What happened?"

"I'm getting married in a few days."

"El, you are many things," he began. "But someone who dives headfirst into something as important as marriage, isn't one of them."

Ellena laughed. His summation of her was true. "You are right, it all happened so suddenly." She went on to explain the circumstances surrounding her upcoming nuptials.

"That's some next level crazy right there," Dro said when she relayed the entire series of event.

She nodded to Saba to let her know it was fine to leave. "I know, right?"

"You, a woman, will be living in the Middle East. Durabia is the bells and whistles of all the great trappings of luxury—the outer appearance of acceptance and inclusion. But there is a dark side, well, darker for you; someone who has lived with American freedoms." He sighed. "Well, what passes as freedom these days, because we have our own issues with racism, bigotry, and a culture that doesn't appreciate women. But these are levels of injustice you grew up with. Something you are well aware of how to maneuver between, to live with it all. Sharia Law is not forgiving. And no amount of love will overcome that. And I don't care how well he laid it on you, El, that's only going to feel good for so long."

Ellena was not happy that he believed these new developments were all mostly about finally having an intimate encounter. There was so much more to their relationship than "slick dick" and "wet ass".

"I know what I'm doing, Dro," she countered, dropping down on the bed. "I appreciate your concern. Really, I do. But I'm marrying Kamran Ali Khan in three days. I simply called because this is less than two weeks' notice."

"I don't care about that," he snapped. "I care about *you*. You've been my right hand, sometimes my left since I opened Vantage Point. You are a valuable employee, but I also consider you family."

Ellena wiped away a tear after hearing these words from a man who had put his life in danger countless times to save his clients. "I know you think I'm being foolish."

"No, you're too headstrong for that," he replied. "What I think is that you're blinded by the good parts—or the good wood—and don't understand how deeply the bad parts can affect you. That's all. I am happy that you have found love. But I want to check this man out; know more about his family." Another rustle of papers on his end. "Give me his full name and I'd like his phone number too."

She lowered herself to the bed. "Dro, don't mess this up for me."

"That is not my plan," he said with a weary sigh. "But I'd like to know how far he's willing to go to make sure you're protected."

"All right."

Dro took down the information. "El, if you don't know anything else, know that I have your back, front, and sides."

"I know that."

"I would like to have Hiram—one of the Knights—place a Castle tattoo on your wrist and his. Ones that match mine."

"Oh, that's really nice of you," she said, relieved that he had found a way to accept the inevitable. Hiram was one of the young men who was being mentored by Dro and his fellow Kings.

"I'll bring him when I come."

Ellena's heart did a leap of joy. "Wait, you're coming for the wedding?"

"Of course. Who else do you think should walk you down the aisle?"

"Victor Alejandro Reyes, I absolutely adore you."

"Well, what's not to adore?" he asked, chuckling before he disconnected the call.

* * *

Dro Reyes walked back into The Castle headquarters mulling over the conversation with El that unsettled him a great deal. Realization dawned that he would have to get the men he trusted with his life involved.

Fate had made them brothers. The efforts they had taken to protect The Castle, each other, and the women they loved. was what made them kings.

His involvement with The Castle started when their mentor and founder of The Castle, Khalil Germaine, ended up on the business end of an assassination attempt. Grant, Alejandro, Shaz, Mariano, Vikkas, Jai, Daron, Kaleb, and Dwayne were snatched from their daily lives and successful businesses in order to right old wrongs and track down the men responsible for trying to kill Khalil.

During the six months when they stepped into the fray, they went through a series of dangerous challenges that altered the path of their lives forever. Not to mention, it also brought on the ire and deadly intent of Castle members—dirty politicians, the Russian mafia, American crime lords, and businessmen with their own sordid agendas—who wielded major influence across the globe.

However, those men were not prepared for the new Kings—also powerful men who brought intelligence, determination, and togetherness in their goal of bringing The Castle back into its original humanitarian purpose.

They had weathered many a challenge, but all of them took place on American soil where they knew the boundaries. The Middle East was an entirely different beast.

"Wheels up, brothers," Dro said, clearing the entrance to the circular boardroom fitted with a range of electronic communications equipment. "Grab your wives or significant others and put a call in to the Knights."

Khalil's olive complexion was slight darker because of his visit to

India a few days ago. He was taller than the average man from that region, fit and still quite muscular for his age. He leveled a dark brown gaze over the rim of his wineglass. "Why?"

"We're going to Durabia."

"Whoa," Shaz said, putting the sandwich he held back onto the plate. "What's going on?"

"El is getting married."

"Wow. Found herself a prince over there, huh?" Vikkas teased with a laugh, reflecting the spitting image of the dark-haired, olive complexion ruggedness of Khalil Germaine.

"Actually, she did."

His smile disappeared and he shared a glance with his twin, Jai. The only difference between them was Jai's silver shock of hair that was in the same place as Khalil's. Jai had weathered a storm of both public and industry censure when a coma patient at his medical center wound up pregnant under mysterious circumstances.

Shaz's head whipped toward Dro, his waist-length locs shifting with the movement. "Seriously?"

"So why does that mean we need to crash the royal wedding?" Jai asked, leaning back in the executive chair.

"El doesn't have family," Dro explained. "I think maybe a niece and a nephew, or two sisters that she keeps in contact with but no one else."

Dro gave his brother Kings Ellena's history. Shared how diligent she had been since he first started Vantage Point right after college. "I need us to be her family. She's in the Middle East, and how they view women—especially Black women—can be dangerous for her."

"No more dangerous than it is here," Jai said, and there was a shadow of sadness in his eyes. Probably reflecting on everything that his coma patient, Temple, had been through.

Dro dropped into his designated seat. "I need the Royal Family to see that she has people who will ride for her. That if anyone thinks they can treat her any kind of way that isn't right, that we will tear that mother—"

Khalil's right eyebrow went up.

"Sorry Khalil." He inhaled, composed himself for a few seconds. "That we will storm that palace and turn their world inside out."

"Are you just angry that you're losing your right hand?" Vikkas asked, his tone holding a humorous note.

Dro shook his head. "I'm disappointed that she didn't give me time to vet him and his family first."

Grant steepled his fingers under his cleft chin. His chiseled face always wore a solemn expression that women considered "brooding" and made it their mission to make him smile. He did, but only with his brothers, family, and the woman he loved. "He's right. There are a lot of great things about Durabia, but there's a darkness there, just like any other country."

"The Royal Family is shielded from *any* wrongdoing." Dro scanned the men at the table with steely eyes. "She could disappear and we wouldn't be able to do a damn thing. I'm not angry about anything. I'm afraid of losing her altogether."

"I've been there twice. All I've seen is lavish malls, exotic restaurants, wonderful entertainment," Vikkas offered. "That's why so many people travel there to shop and play."

"And that's the only part they advertise," Daron said, returning his glass to the table. "I've been there as well. The place is under Sharia Law. El doesn't know anything about that. At least here, there is some recourse when something is done wrong—not much, but enough."

"Women are seen as having half the value of men—even in their word when it comes to legal issues," Grant said, finally lifting his eyes from the screen in front of him. "Their death by the hands of a man, or even being raped by one, won't bring justice. Men are given a wide berth."

"Same as right here in America," Vikkas, an international lawyer, said as Shaz, an immigration and family lawyer, gave a nod.

Dro took that in, then added, "At least we know how to function within our laws, as unjust and slanted as they may be. She doesn't have anything to protect her there."

Dwayne, an educator who had embraced and executed Khalil's methods of teaching students and soon to be princes of The Castle, slid his tablet into a leather briefcase. "I need to schedule one of the Knights to keep tabs on things at the school. When do we leave?"

"Tonight." Dro nodded, a plan already formulating in his mind. "Tonight works for me."

"Brother, you're not playing," Kaleb, a real estate magnate in Detroit, said with a chuckle.

"Not even a little bit."

"I would like to come as well."

All eyes shifted to Khalil.

Dro was honored that their mentor would involve himself in such a simple domestic issue. "Khalil, you don't have to do that."

"But I must," he insisted and his tone did not leave room for any argument.

Dro peered at him, taking in the solemn set of his expression. "I don't understand."

Khalil stood, moving around the table until he was closer to Dro. "Part of the reason my family was so willing to force me out was the unhealthy competition for wealth with the Khan family."

Vikkas perked up, and so did Jai, who asked, "You're related to them?"

"Yes, I am."

"In what way?" Dwayne asked.

"Sheikh Aayan of the House Maharaj is my uncle."

"Six degrees of separation, huh?" Grant said, over his glass of Hershey's Porter beer.

"Not so separate anymore," Khalil countered. "Shall I prepare to join you?"

"Of course," Dro said as Khalil made his way to the doorway. "This should prove to be very interesting."

Khalil paused at the exit. "Trust me, you do not know the half of it."

Chapter 19

"Kamran speaking."

Even with two words, the man's voice was the kind that made people take notice. Dro shifted the phone against his ear. "I am Alejandro Reyes."

"Yes, Ellena said you wish to speak with me."

Dro scanned the dossier on the Khan family that was spread out on his desk. "What are your true intentions towards El?"

"I am marrying her because she is an amazing woman."

"But you didn't know her from Eve's cat over a week ago."

"Who is Eve?"

Dro exhaled, trying not to slap a hand to his forehead. The background noise on Kamran's end didn't hide the innocence in that question.

"Just joking," Kamran said with a throaty chuckle. "And you are correct, I did not. But it is God's will that we are together. She is my gift from God, not the other way around."

Dro spun to an image of Sheikh Aayan Khan on the pages of a

tabloid. "I've done a little research on your family."

"And you will find that my family is one of the richest in the world. We have been plagued by our share of drama, more than others. My father has six wives. Well, soon to be five since one wife is now seeking asylum and a forced marriage protection in England. She does not wish her daughters to be married to any of the Nadaum princes."

"I will find all of that out," Dro countered, flipping to yet another page detailing where a Durabian princess had run away from home. "No worries."

"Alejandro, we both want what is best for Ellena, yes?"

"Facts."

"My best is to show her the love and respect that she deserves," he said, moving to a quieter area. "Do you know she defied the Sheikh and nearly tossed me back because she felt it was unfair that she was forced on me as a wife instead of it being my choice."

Dro smiled. "That sounds a lot like El."

"That is the moment I fell in love with her," he confessed. "No one has *ever* stood up for me the way she has. She is filled with compassion, determination, courage."

"That is El, too," Dro conceded.

"Those nine days that I took to court her, it was about getting to know her. But in doing so, I learned more about myself. She made me question my life and my faith. Made me see things I have accepted as normal that I have done nothing to change. Marriage to her is more than a gift, it is a blessing for my life. I could not have prayed for a better woman." The man's voice sounded sincere. "I will not be able to do as much as I would like here in Durabia to take on the elements that are wrong, but we will find a way to try. Now what is your true concern?"

"That she will be harmed by things that are out of her control because the culture is not part of her life."

"We have already determined that," he countered. "And she changed the Sheikh's mind with a plan to remain here. But we will reside in the Free Zone, not the palace."

Way to go, El! "Well, that puts a different spin on things. So, she will not be under the shadow of Sharia Law?"

"No, only with a weekly visit for dinner at the palace and I think she will manage quite well. I believe my father is smitten with her himself. I heard him say to my brother that she would have made an excellent seventh wife."

"That makes me feel better, I think." *Seventh wife?*

"I am glad to hear it." Dro typed a message to Shaz, Jai, and Vikkas on his cell phone. "And you know what else will make me feel better?"

"Ask, and I will do my best."

"But you cannot mention a word of it to Ellena."

"I will not keep secrets from my wife."

Dro nodded, pleased by that assertion. "I am glad to hear it, but once you listen to what I'm asking, I think you will agree to this one."

Chapter 20

"Who gives this woman—"

"We do," blasted from every corner of the palace ballroom. A group of men and women seemed to appear out of nowhere, gliding toward where Ellena stood. The Durabian guests parted to give them clear access across the patterned marble floor. The room had been transformed into a wonderland of lilac, purple, creams, and golds—flowers galore.

Sheikh Aayan craned his neck around Kamran so he could see who had spoken. "And who are you?"

Murmurs began, then climbed in a rousing crescendo around the palace, but came to a halt when the first man in line stepped forward and said, "Victor Alejandro Reyes. King of Hyde Park."

"Shastra Bostwick, King of Evanston," a tall loc-wearing man said before another man with a light complexion came abreast of him. "Daron Kincaid, King of Morgan Park," he said.

"Kaleb Valentine, King of South Shore," was spoken by a man with tight curls and brown skin, followed by, "Grant Khambrel, King of Lincoln Park." This one had dark, brooding eyes which was a stark contrast to the man standing next to him, who almost seemed to be of

East Indian descent. "Dwayne Harper, King of Lawndale," and then another with ivory skin and piercing dark eyes, said, "Mariano Francesco DeLuca."

The last two standing on the front line looked as though they could be direct members of Kamran's family.

"Jaidev Maharaj Germaine, of the House of Maharaj seated in the United States of America and empire of India, King of Devon."

Sheikh Aayan blanched, seemingly disturbed by this sudden turn of events.

"Vikkas Maharaj Germaine of the House of Maharaj seated in the United States of America and empire of India, King of Wilmette."

The introductions didn't end there as Kings led into "Milan Germaine of the House of Maharaj seated in the United States of America and empire of India, Queen of Wilmette."

"Cameron Stone, Queen of Morgan Park."

"Temple Germaine of the House of Maharaj seated in the United States of America and empire of India, Queen of Devon."

"Camilla Bostwick, Queen of Evanston by way of the Parish of St. Catherine, Jamaica, West Indies."

All followed by the rest of the Queens, then, "Hiram Fosten, Knight of Grand Crossing," before the remaining eight Knights and their significant others, the princes and princesses all addressed the court.

The Kings were distinguished in long white tunics—the same dishdashas as the men in Kamran's family, but the American Kings had an embroidered crown crest on the upper right part of their chest. Each wore golden crowns that were as imposing as the men themselves. The Knights were formidable in black, the princes decked in red, with all queens, ladies, princesses robed in magnificent garments in colors that complimented the men. The image they presented was nothing short of spectacular. Kamran was duly impressed and actually felt a little chuffed that his father had been thrown off his square.

Then one man of regal bearing, with silky salt-and-pepper hair, an expertly trimmed goatee, draped in full East Indian garb, said, "I am Khalil Germaine, formerly Masood Ali Khan Maharaj of the East Indian Maharaj family line from Bihar, Mauryans, Delhi Sultanate, and Mughal Empires. And we lay claim to Ellena Kiley as a daughter, sister, each in kind. Her dowry—bride price—one million from each king, and nine million from the House of Maharaj America."

Sheikh Aayan nearly fell backward onto the throne. As well he should. Ellena's dowry was the most that any of the princesses that were married to his brothers had brought to the table. Substantially more. "I thought she was a commoner," he said, his voice carrying throughout the room, but he glared at Kamran as though accusing him of keeping this vital information to himself.

"No more common than anyone here," Khalil responded with a smile. "The difference is bloodline, family, and money—of which she has plenty."

He let that comment walk around the room for a moment and it caused all others to resume their curiosity-filled conversations.

Kamran locked gazes with Alejandro and gave him a head nod. All the Kings answered with an approving nod of their own—in unison. Kamran leaned over to Ellena and asked, "Is this where the big guy comes in and sings she's your queen to be?"

"I'm going to put you over my knee," she whispered through her teeth, trying to hold back laughter at his reference to the movie, *Coming to America.*

"Go to Khalil," Kamran said, smiling. "He will walk you back to my side as is the custom for a father offering his daughter."

"Wait, is that Dolly and Damaris," she asked, as her heart swelled with joy. "The Kings, the Knights, the Queens, my classmates. You knew?"

"I knew they would come," he replied. "I did not know *this*." His gaze scanned her family. "But take a gander at my brother's faces."

Shock, panic, and major concern were among the range of expressions.

"Priceless."

"You walk back to me. And you hold your head high, do you hear me? Your family has put everyone here on notice—including me—that you are not to be trifled with. That you are not a motherless or fatherless child. That there are those who will stand for you when you cannot stand for yourself. And more importantly"—his voice deepened—"anyone who comes for you will lose their lives. Message received. Hold your head up, my queen."

Her eyes glazed over with tears.

Kamran kissed the first one that fell.

Then Ellena glided to Khalil, who extended his arm and brought hers under his before he placed a kiss on her forehead.

"I present to you," Khalil said in a voice that carried to every corner of the ballroom. "Ellena Kiley Maharaj, of the House of Maharaj seated in the United States of America and empire of India."

Chapter 21

"Ellena, I have been to many a wedding over the years," Kamran said, closing the door to their palace suite, which had been decorated with flowers and décor from the wedding, so the theme of happiness carried throughout. They would leave for America tomorrow to honeymoon and tie up her business and family endeavors there. But tonight, as was the required custom, they would remain in Durabia. "By far, this was the best one—ever."

She turned amused eyes on him. "You're just saying that because it's our wedding."

"No, my love. I am saying it because it is true." He did a little dance. "We learned to Salsa, and what was the other dance?"

Ellena sat on the bed and slid off her heels. "Stepping. Chicago style stepping."

"Yes, and Kizomba. They brought instructors." He pretended to dance with an imaginary Ellena. "They took over the whole wedding.

My family lost their entire minds. I love it!"

She laughed at his entertaining attempt to get the moves it would take him more than a night to master.

"And what is the name of that song they played for us again?"

"The Makings of You," she replied.

The love song was the same one that her classmates had remixed for Kamran and Ellena's dance during the class reunion dinner. Both versions—Gladys Knight and Curtis Mayfield—had been blended to lengthen the track as Kamran led Ellena in a slow dance. Only later did she find out that he had requested for Dolly, Damaris, Ronnie and David to teach him the movements. She was shocked and impressed. The joyful tears that pooled in her eyes were his reward.

"I think your family may have had more fun than they expected," Ellena said. "Your sisters were all sourpusses before my family arrived. But when they came out there to learn the dances … did you see them?"

"I saw them," Kamran said, laughing. "Your family, they were fierce. Most impressive to have the world-renowned Khalil Germaine stand in as your father. He even brought a signed certificate of your claim of belonging to the Germaine-Maharaj family. Woman, you have been holding out on me."

She gasped and held up her hand. "I promise you, I didn't—"

"I know, my love," he said, kissing the tip of her nose. "Alejandro explained some of what would happen. Actually, only a small amount. He asked me to find a seamstress to sew the crest onto each garment— and the colors and sizes, but the image they presented—how do you say it—badass."

Ellena grinned. "What do you know about that?"

"Well, I consider myself a little bit of a badass," he replied, popping an imaginary collar.

"That you are, Kamran Ali Khan."

They shared a kiss and when he pulled away, he told her, "And just so you know, I think Dolly and Rashid might be the next ones down the aisle."

"Seriously?"

"Yes. And we will be seeing more of your brothers."

"How so?" she asked, making her way to the bathroom.

"Each one of the Kings, Knights, and a few of the Queens put in applications to open a business here."

She poked her head out. "Are you serious?"

"Yes, I am very sure." He gave an affirmative nod with his answer. "They need a local sponsor for that."

Ellena slid into the silk robe that Saba had placed on the massive bed. "I don't understand."

"Only Nationals can start a business here. Anyone else must have a National sponsor them. And that sponsor is paid a fee and owns fifty-one percent of the business."

She moved closer to him, perched on the chaise as she pondered that for a few moments. "So, who will be my brothers' sponsors?"

Kamran winked, and Ellena chuckled.

"Business will cause them to travel to and from Durabia," Kamran said, as he crossed the distance between them and settled beside her. "But the real reason is they want to keep tabs on you …" He paused a moment as her face crumpled. "Oh, my love, do not cry. I did not say that to make you sad."

"I'm not sad," she said between sniffles. "These are tears of joy. How did I go from a woman with only a few family members that matter to like … a whole army of them? I never realized how lonely my life was until I saw all of these people here wishing me well and promising to stay in touch. And they were sincere. Every one of them. And then Melissa was here. Ah! Thank you so much. I only wish my sister, Amanda could come, but Christian had the brilliant idea to do a live video exchange so she was able to see everything and even say a few words to me."

He eased one arm around Ellena and kissed her ear. "And why couldn't she come?"

"Legally, she still can't leave the country," Ellena said. "Long story. Involves my mother, who screwed up royally—no pun intended—and Amanda ended up on the wrong end of two bodies."

"Wait. What?" Kamran's smooth brows came together in a frown.

"Later," she shot back. "It's too much to get into right now." Then she averted her gaze to the open window. "I know Grant and Kaleb are into real estate, so they might buy some property."

His lips pressed into a thin line.

She narrowed a gaze on him. "What?"

"They cannot buy property here. Only a National can," he admitted. "They are only able to lease it for ninety-nine years. My father wanted to ensure that Durabia did not end up like America and Africa. So many parts of it are owned by people who were not born there. Your America, the bridges, the roads, they are not owned by your government."

Ellena thought that over for a few seconds and was floored. "I didn't know that."

"Most do not. And do not be alarmed." He took her hand in his. "We are not the only country that protects our land and economy that way."

She peered at him, and he could tell that information still did not sit too well. "But you all depend on eighty-five percent of the labor from outside. I looked at the landscape, Kamran. Fifty percent of the skyline is mostly cranes in the middle of construction. You all are building far beyond your ability to sustain the city yourselves." She gave him a side-eye as she expounded, "If everyone decided that Durabia was no longer the place to work and people stop coming, what would happen?"

When he didn't answer, she continued, "So, it is the play capital for Nationals, then your family reaps of all the benefits and live in luxury while everyone else works to build it and suffer. Sounds so much like America."

She expressed the same point he had been making to his father for years, but it still sounded harsher coming from Ellena.

Kamran rubbed his temples. "My love, we are not going to have a cultural, social conscious, or political debate on our wedding night."

"All right." Ellena gave an adult version of a pout and snatched her hands out of his. She folded both arms across her breasts. Goodness knows those luscious brown nipples were calling his name and he wanted to be feasting on them right now.

"All right, my love," he conceded with a weary sigh. "Speak your piece."

Her shoulder tensed, then she went all in with, "I can understand the point of making Durabia the best destination for the entire world, but what are you doing to help others who are less fortunate?"

"My love, there is no poverty here," he protested.

"Right, because if people aren't working for your family's benefit or bringing money into this economy, they aren't even allowed to be here."

"Checks and balances," Kamran shot back, now becoming concerned. "They make more money here than at home."

"And they have to live twelve to an apartment to sustain that," she countered, glancing around their luxurious bedroom. "Where is the fairness in that? And then there's a place where men from all over the globe frequent. Girls have been brought over here to service men. *Girls*, not women."

Kamran inhaled sharply. This was another point he had made numerous times to his father. To no avail. "It is a necessary evil that has existed for centuries. How do you expect it to change?"

"You might not be able to, but I expect you—*for us*—to try. Every girl needs to feel the way I did today. That they have someone looking out for them. That someone cares. Why can't you be that someone?"

Kamran gave that much thought. An organization in the neighboring country of Dubai offered a safe haven for women and girls who had fallen prey to men who put them to work in the sex industry. They could emulate all of their work in Durabia, but the backlash would be epic. The way Ellena was looking at him made him want to win her approval. "We will try."

She embraced him. "And speaking of trying ... you set the bar our first time making love. So I'm expecting that to be your norm."

"Oh, the pressure." He did a dramatic hand slap to the forehead.

"I'm just saying." She tweaked his nose. "Now that we're married, don't start having headaches and whatnot."

"You are laying it on pretty thick, are you not?"

Her eyes danced as she laughed. "I mean. I'd like for you to lay it on me pretty thick. Enough talk."

"Wife," he said, shocked at the forwardness, though he shouldn't be. "Husband."

Ellena straddled his lap.

"Why do I have a feeling that a little Marvin Gaye should be playing in the background?" he asked, burying his head in the fullness of her breasts.

"Because he always had the right idea," she countered. "Let's get it on."

Chapter 22

Amir walked into his palace suite and froze when he laid eyes on Faiza. The morning hours before the break of dawn normally found his wife stretched out over the bed, poised as if no one should touch her. He rarely did. Once when he tried to initiate sex, she told him, "I'm not an animal. You will not rut on me like I'm a brood mare."

Her attitude was one of the reasons he visited El Zalaam so often. At least he could have his needs fulfilled elsewhere.

"I want to see it," she commanded.

He ignored her outstretched hand. "Not possible."

"I *demand* to see it."

Amir shook his head, then passed on the right side of the bed. "I do not wish for my wife to put eyes on such a thing."

She stewed for several moments, then a sly smile graced her red lips. "It is all right. I will ask Salman or Umar. They will have no such reservations."

Amir whipped around to face her. "But then they will know I told you something that I should not have."

"Yes, they will." She grinned and it was not a good look for her. Her hand was out again. "Let me see it."

He pulled out his cell, trudged to Faiza and queued up the video.

"On your phone, no less," she said, her voice dripping with disdain.

Faiza snatched it from his hands, watching the first visuals of Kamran and Ellena's wedding night at the palace. After a few minutes, she inched backwards, dropping down onto the nearest chair. Her eyes remained glued to the screen, mouth forming a small "oh" at times, others rated a jaw drop.

Almost an eternity later, Amir finally plucked his phone from her trembling hands, though the video was still playing. The wives seemed to have some code they lived by. Give just enough attention to their husband to get with child, then distance themselves from anything related to sex.

Faiza's shell-shocked expression was all the excuse he needed to play on her curiosity. Now, maybe she would stop giving him grief about his visits to El Zalaam, or readily submit herself to doing what it took to please him.

His father had taught him that men should indulge in anything they could afford. He could count the times that luxury cars were abandoned because owners had run up a tab before that next wave of money came in. Most of the rich didn't have to work, so it was easy to become lazy and let life unfold as it came. Royals had a never-ending source of money. Whatever they couldn't purchase outright, they had someone procure, whether legally or illegally.

He smiled. Though he had been reluctant to allow her into the wicked exploits of Kamran and Ellena, this could be a win for him.

"So," he said, claiming the space next to her, before stroking her arm. "What do you think? "

Faiza shrugged him off, saying, "I think I married the wrong brother."

Chapter 23

"Grandma, you were not invited," Blair Swanson said, alarmed that her carefully executed farewell dinner for Auntie Ellena was about to be ruined by the one woman no one cared to see. Ruth Hinton stood squarely in the entrance of Blair's house in the heart of Jeffrey Manor on the southeast side of Chicago.

"I don't care," the wig-wearing woman said, trying to push past Blair, who squarely planted her feet and stood her ground. "I want to see her. I *demand* to see her."

"I promised she wouldn't have to see you," Blair warned. "That's the only reason she's here."

"That's not my problem," Ruth snapped. "You shouldn't have told her that."

Blair repositioned her athletic body to block the way. "I'm going to have to ask you to leave. Now."

Ruth reared back as though she was about to lay hands on Blair. "Or what? You're going to call the police?"

"I shouldn't have to." Blair angled again, completely blocking the doorway. "Please leave."

"Oh, let her come in," Dorsey demanded, pushing Blair away from the threshold. "It's not going to kill Ellena to see her own mother."

"Unfortunate choice of words, Auntie," Blair snapped, and saw Dorsey and her twin Dorothy flinch.

She gave a dismissive wave and said, "You know what I meant."

"Come on in, Mama," Dorothy said, glaring at Blair as Katrina, Katherine and Klara looked on, but obviously from their sour expressions, the triplets were on Dorothy's side. "Ignore all this foolishness. It's time she got over it anyhow."

Blair stepped into Dorothy's space in the foyer. The modest living room and dining area were already overflowing with family from her father's side and only two from her mother's—just to keep the peace.

"How the hell are you going to tell someone else when they should be over the death of four children? That man paid Grandma to take her children so he wouldn't have to pay child support. They're dead because of her greed and his." Blair tilted her head as she peered at the shorter woman, whose careworn face was evidence of the battle scars she'd suffered in life. "If she had done that to you, would you be so willing to let it go?" She waited a couple of beats before adding, "Didn't think so."

"What's going on? I am—" Ellena and Christian walked into the living room from the dining area and laid eyes on Ruth. She tipped backwards and put a hand to her chest, gasping. Kamran supported her from the other side, his face filled with concern.

Blair was by her side, almost in tears as she tried to make sure her aunt didn't faint from the shock of seeing the woman she had every reason to hate. "Auntie, I swear I didn't—"

"I know." Ellena flickered a gaze to Dorsey, who wore a smirk that spoke volumes. "I know exactly who did it. She's been hinting at it since I arrived."

Blair beckoned for Christian to come forward. Her favorie cousin was immediately by her side.

"Auntie Ellena," Blair whispered. "I'll understand if you can't stay."

"It's been nine years. Enough already," Veda shrieked, throwing up her weathered hands.

"I agree," Rolanda, Veda's twin, said in a soft voice, her short cap of curls barely framing her round face. "You're here and maybe we can heal."

"And how many children do you have?" Auntie Amanda snapped, tilting her head.

Nothing but silence as Rolanda's gaze fell to the carpet. Amanda normally was the quiet one. Blair felt honored that Amanda and Ellena were taking her side.

Ruth had stolen money from Christian and Blair that had been slated to secure Amanda's release from a restitution center in the South. Ruth had taken a call that was meant for Blair, used the information, and what resulted was an unfortunate series of events that still impacted Amanda to this day.

Amanda, like Ellena, had distanced herself from all the members of the family except Blair and her mother, Lela, Christian and his mother, Melissa. Things had become so toxic from Blair's paternal side of the family tree, it resulted in the need for two separate Thanksgivings, two separate Christmas events, and most major holidays.

"Don't talk to me about healing," Ellena snapped at Rolanda while stepping away from Kamran. "I forgave her a long time ago, but forgetting is another thing entirely."

"Well, if you don't forget, then you don't forgive," Veda quipped.

"Not true," Kamran countered, coming to Ellena's side, placing his arm about her waist.

Dorsey waved her hands in his face. "Hey, we didn't ask for your opinion, Swami."

Kamran honed in on the brash woman and said, "When it comes to my wife, I will give *every* opinion that matters. She does not wish to be reminded of the most painful time of her life. And that is her right. As her husband, it is my duty to protect her from harm, even if it comes under the guise of family."

"And you put your hands in his face again," Ellena warned Dorsey. "I will whip your entire ass."

Kamran stepped around, moving until he stood in front of Ellena so she didn't make good on that threat. "Come, my love. Let us take our leave. Blair, Amanda, Christian, by all means, please come to Ellena's home later tonight. We have gifts to impart to you and your children. And bring Lela and Melissa as well."

"What about our gifts?" Klara demanded, eyes rolling toward the ceiling.

"She just arrived," Kamran said with a charming smile while gesturing to Ruth. "She will remain and we will give you all the space to enjoy her presence. I think that is your gift. We bid you peace." He tossed up the sideways peace sign he'd seen Ellena throw up a few times.

Blair shared a speaking glance with Christian, who cracked up laughing.

"Kamran, do I say like … Sheikh, king, your highness or anything like that?" Blair asked, still trying to contain her laughter.

"You are family," he answered. "Kamran is fine."

"Do they have hospitals in Durabia that would hire surgical scrub techs from America?"

Kamran looked at Ellena for a moment and she nodded before he said, "I will see to it. You wish to work in Durabia?"

"With all this unnecessary drama, I think my immediate family needs a change and better opportunities," Blair admitted, going to the foyer closet and retrieving several coats. "Sometimes I fear for my children's safety. Little girls are coming up missing every day, and women too. And Christian's been stopped by the police so many times we had to get a dash cam to protect him. I just don't feel Chicago is safe for women, especially Black women. Actually, I don't feel safe anywhere in America, given who's in office for that matter."

"So, you're just going to up and leave here on some type of maybe?" Veda snarled. "How dumb is that? Those headrag-wearing folks. They ain't no better. They kill people over there. *Especially* women. Get out of line and see what happens. Am I right, Kammy?"

"Kamran," he corrected. "And Blair, just like my wife, will not be under Sharia Law. She will live in the Free Zone in the same locale as we do."

"That's what's up," Christian said. "Any room for brothers with brand management, graphic design, and photography skills? Chicago is becoming an interesting place for Black men. Actually, America in general is becoming an interesting place for all people to tell the truth, but we're having a tougher time than most."

"You are *not* going to the Middle East," Melissa cried, with her eyes flashing defiance. "Who's going to take care of me?"

"Mama, you can take care of yourself. If there are opportunities there for employment, then I need to try. At least we have someone who can guide us to the right places, and I can send money here to help take care of things. Then, when you're comfortable, you can come and live with me."

She took that in for a moment her expression more sorrowful than hopeful; and nodded as the rest of the family filed into the room; making the space tighter than it already was.

"But who's going to watch me come in late at night," Melissa protested. "You're always … you always come over when you know I'm going to make it in late. Sometimes you're at my house when I get in just to make sure I'm safe. Do you know how wonderful that makes me feel?"

Christian embraced his mother. "Mama, I'll have a flood light with a camera installed out back. And I'll see you come in. It'll even allow me to talk or say something to alert you that you're in danger." He embraced her as tears slid down her face. "It'll be all right."

Veda put a hand on her fleshy hips. "So this Arabian sand ni—"

"Hey," Christian snapped. "Watch it. You don't want folks calling us that, so don't call him that."

Klara's lips curled into a snarl and finished with the words Veda meant to say. "Just walks up in here and takes our children like some Swami Pied Piper."

"Did she just try to call me the N-word?" Kamran asked Blair, frowning. "I thought people aren't supposed to say that?"

"Long story about *some* people using it," Christian replied, glaring at Veda.

"And she's wrong for saying that about you," Blair added.

Veda sauntered up to Kamran. "Well, if you're going to take somebody, take the rest of us, too, partner. You're rolling in it, you might as well make it a family affair."

"The difference is, Blair and Christian asked for employment," Ellena said, barely hanging on to her temper as she pushed herself between them. "You're looking for a free ride on our dime and that will happen when hell freezes over and we can all ice skate across."

Chapter 24

A few months later, Ellena peered into the bathroom where Kamran was taking a shower and singing at the top of his lungs. "Are you in here belting out Luther?"

He cracked open the glass door, peered out, and gave her a sheepish grin.

"Oh, my word," she said, doubling over with laughter. "Who have you been hanging out with?"

"Your brothers. They arrived yesterday for a series of meetings about the businesses they are establishing here."

Ellena passed him a bath sheet from the metal warmer. "What kind of business?"

Kamran flipped through his mental Rolodex before he shared the extent of their recent projects. A rehab facility, a medical center focused on at-risk children, domestic violence and sex trafficking victim shelters, education centers focused on world economy and humanitarian service orientation. Then there was the fact that Kamran now had daily meetings with his father to discuss implementing some of the plans he had laid on the table. A great deal of them resulted in putting more money in Kamran's account, as well as land ownership and intellectual property. His brothers were becoming increasingly jealous and concerned. But the Sheikh made sure that Kamran was fairly situated and compensated for his efforts—regardless of how anyone else felt. The only bone of contention was Ellena's center for women. Ever since the property was purchased and she had started the process of rescuing women from El Zalaam, the men in his family were in an uproar. Kamran could care less.

"That's amazing," she said, narrowing her gaze on him. "So what else have they been up to?"

"I love their ideas, and I like Khalil. Dro and Daron are here working with the Knights. Two of the princes—scholars from a place called Excel—are supposed to come on Spring Break. They are going to prepare for having university level education here. They also brought in Hiram and Larry Tankson for martial arts training; and Daron and Dro are giving them weapons trainings. And I will as well." He curled his arms about her. "I would like you to have weapons training."

"Absolutely not," was the beginning of a long, heated diatribe against the use of guns of any kind. Especially given what had happened with her sister, Amanda.

Kamran listened patiently and when she paused to draw a breath, he said, "Can I have my head back now?"

Ellena blew out a breath before squinting at him. "Who did you get *that* from?"

"Kaleb Valentine. Each of your brothers imparted valuable relationship advice on dealing with a Black woman as a mate. Kaleb warned that there will be times when you go off the deep end of the argument and I need to apologize and ask for my head back because you will have officially chopped it off. Verbally speaking." He nodded, then smiled, obviously proud of himself for remembering.

She chuckled and said, "I'm sorry. I should not have gone off on you that way."

"See? It works." He left the seat and did a little Salsa and his smile was wider than the Durabia River.

"I am going to forbid you from being with my brothers."

The dance halted and his smile instantly disappeared. "Do not do that."

"You like them, huh?"

"They act more brotherly toward me than the ones related by blood." Kamran stroked the tattoo Hiram Fosten had inked high up his wrists. "I admire who they are and what they stand for. Khalil …" He shook his head, remembering the deep conversations he had with the man whose vision was nothing short of amazing. "If only my father would listen to him, Durabia would be on the path of being not only the epicenter of trade, oil, tourism, and medical advancements, we would be a world leader in peace."

"World peace. I like the sound of that. He is an amazing man," Ellena agreed.

"Yes, and he knows how to use a weapon, too," Kamran slid in with a suggestive lift of his eyebrows.

"All right. All right. I will do it."

"Thank you. And soon, please." He frowned as he pulled her onto his lap and the towel slid lower around his waist. "Although, on second thought, you being able to handle a weapon might be a dangerous thing."

She moved her hips in a circular motion. "Well, there's one weapon I'm pretty good with."

Chapter 25

"What in the entire hell?" Ellena shrieked loud enough to shake the hanging certificates in the doctor's office.

"Pregnant?" Kamran said, slowly getting to his feet.

The doctor shrank back a little.

"My wife is pregnant?"

The woman pointed to the top of the page facing them. "Yes, your Highness, about three months along."

"And this is not a game or a prank?"

"No, sir," she answered him, her expression grave. "She is very much with child."

Kamran's shocked expression was reflected in Ellena's as she patiently waited for him to question the paternity also. That seemed to be the norm when a man was shocked with such news, especially when he believed he couldn't give a woman a child. Ellena had several bouts of nausea that resulted in multiple trips to the chamber and a loss of appetite, plus a little weight gain. Kamran insisted that she see a physician who ran tests.

He dropped down into the chair. "I'm not sterile?"

"Whoever made that original assertion, without testing your sperm, I might add, made a grave error," Dr. Gupta said, narrowing her gaze on Kamran. "It could've been timing. Maybe pregnancies occurred and miscarried before you even realized. So many factors."

"Or they could've been taking preventative measures to avoid one as well," Ellena said.

"Not possible," Dr. Gupta explained with a pointed look at Ellena. "Birth control is not allowed for Royals or women who are expected to produce children."

"That is a misconception and I would appreciate if you would not perpetuate it any further," Kamran said. "Due to the need for population control, Islam does permit the use of contraceptives to prevent pregnancy, to treat menstrual disorders, and to suppress menstrual flow that would prevent attendance at religious rituals. Only lately has the wrong belief that Islamic law prohibits contraception been spreading." He shifted his focus to his wife. "Ellena, my love, how could you not know? Didn't you—"

"No, my cycle has always had a mind of its own. If it came, fine, if it didn't—no big deal. It's not like I was whoring for a living and had to worry about it."

The doctor's lips lifted at the corners as Kamran grimaced.

"I'm not sterile," he whispered. A smile spread on his face that was so wide she could stick a sail in it and push it off to sea. Then as though suddenly remembering she was in the room, he focused on her. "My love, how are you feeling about this?"

"I'm certainly not about to do cartwheels," she replied, and didn't think he realized that with this news, the five-year expiration date on their marriage had been unexpectedly extended—whether she wanted it to or not. "This won't be an easy thing. I'm no spring chicken."

"But you are no old cluck, either," he countered with a tilt of his head.

She parted her lips to give a comeback, but said, "That was funny."

"Will she be able to sustain a healthy pregnancy?" he asked, focusing on the doctor, who chuckled at their exchange. "I mean, how will this affect her health overall?"

"She's in pretty decent condition."

"What am I? A used car or something?" Ellena shot back, frowning.

"We have to watch her blood pressure and she's borderline diabetic, which can become an issue as the months pass." Dr. Gupta steepled manicured fingers under her angular face, then glanced down at the chart. "Any complications from your previous pregnancies?"

"No, it was pretty smooth going, considering I was carrying four."

Dr. Gupta's head whipped toward Ellena. "Four children? At one time?"

"Yes, quadruplets." Ellena tore her gaze away from the doctor and focused on the garden right outside the window. "I have a genetic condition, a predisposition to hyper-ovulate, which means releasing multiple eggs in one cycle, which significantly increases the chance of having multiples. All of my sisters have it. My mother gave birth to eleven children. One son, ten girls, mostly twins and triplets."

Dr. Gupta typed that information into the electronic chart. "That means more than likely you'll carry more than one child this time as well."

"Will that make things worse?" Kamran asked, taking Ellena's hand in his. "Put more pressure on her body? How can we be sure that she is all right?" His hold tightened on her hand until she could almost feel his anxiety. "I do not wish to lose my wife because she is carrying my child—or my children."

"We will monitor her very closely," Dr. Gupta said, offering a reassuring smile.

"Pregnant," he whispered and the slow smile that graced his face was worth withholding her real fears. Then his expression turned solemn. *Here we go. The paternity question.*

"You seem worried."

"I am," he admitted. "I do not think you understand."

"Understand what?"

"Your pregnancy is going to turn the Royal Palace on its head. My whole life had changed because of this one factor …"

* * *

Seventeen years ago . . ..

"My son, it is with a heavy heart that I must announce that Amir will be the next in line for the throne."

Shocked gasps went up from every corner of the dining room.

Kamran's fork paused midway to his mouth, his mind flipped through a number of scenarios. "Father, you could always appoint a successor after me."

"Yes, but what message does it send to the Muslim world to have a king on the throne who is not virile? Unable to produce heirs of his own? We cannot be seen as weak," he said, waving off the servant who tried to refill his glass. "It is regretful that this change is necessary, but Amir will ascend as Crown Prince and you will become my royal advisor."

The world went into a mighty spin on its axis as Kamran tried to process this life-altering decision. The snide remarks, the not-quite-hidden laughter, the accusing eyes, the elation in the faces of his brothers' wives—all registered at once. His father could have done this in private first before announcing this ... demotion to everyone, including visiting royalty.

Kamran stood, tried hard to ignore the jeers and whispered conversations. He didn't miss the joy in Amir, Laraib, Nadam, Salman, and Umar's faces and knew they would be in a heated competition for their father's favor. Kamran had two former wives, both of them believed to be barren until they were sent home and somehow produced several children with men who were not of a Royal line. His heart was so heavy at being rejected by his father as a result of what transpired with those two women of the Nadaum Kingdom, that he went to the men's prayer room to communicate with God. "Allah, why has thou brought me to this place?"

"My son," Farah whispered and lowered herself to his side, having entered a place forbidden to her and all women. "We never know what Allah plans for us. I know your life path was on the throne, but this actually gives you freedom." She stroked his hair before trailing her hand down his face.

"But at what cost?"

"Your sanity," she said. "You are no longer bound by the restrictions that come with being crowned. You can live your life the way you desire. Do not look on this as a horrible measure."

Kamran absorbed her words, but shame filled him all over again. He had failed his family and would never see Durabia realize the full potential he envisioned. "I love you, Mama. But right now, I cannot see the good in any of this."

"You will, my son. You will."

* * *

Dr. Gupta answered a call and when she replaced the receiver on the cradle, she said, "Your father has summoned both of you to the palace."

"Yes, I am certain he has." Kamran stood, knowing that the doctor had already done what was required—informing the palace that a new royal was on the way. "Just so that we are clear, if it harms her health, we will terminate the pregnancy. I can be without a child, but I will not be without my wife. Do you understand?"

Dr. Gupta blanched at the directive, which was totally against the norm. She was well aware that protecting the life of the mother was regarded as a lesser evil in deciding who lived and who died. The mother was the 'originator' of the fetus and her life was already well-established, while the fetus was merely a possibility of a life until it made it past the womb. Durabians also believed that the mother had duties and responsibilities to attend to when it came to her husband and family. And in many cases, allowing the mother to die would also kill the fetus.

Kamran leaned against the desk so his face was closer. "So that we are clear. If at any point, this pregnancy poses a danger to Ellena, it is my wife over my unborn children."

"Yes, Your Highness," she said, and her tone was filled with concern. "Are you certain?"

"Most definitely."

Chapter 26

"That old camel is pregnant? Pregnant!" Faiza screamed. "Do you know how unbelievable that is?"

Their palace suite was in disarray. His wife had tossed nearly everything in her closet about the room. The place looked more like a bomb had been set off in her closet, leaving an array of colors and garments strewn in every direction—the bed, the floor, the bathroom. He could barely see the intricate floral patterns in the purple and gold carpet.

"Calm down," Amir said, grasping her shoulders as she paced past him for the hundredth time. "So, she's going to whip out a puppy. What does it matter? They are half breeds. They will not ascend to the throne. Neither will he."

"Then you are not paying attention," she snarled. "Kamran has your father's ear. All of a sudden he is implementing businesses and programs with those fake American Kings, Queens, and blasted Knights. None of it has anything to do with you." She jabbed a finger in his chest.

"I'm telling you that Ellena Maharaj becoming pregnant is going to be a major problem." She pulled out of his reach and slammed her hand against the nearest wall. "The whole reason Kamran was passed over for the throne is because he could not sire a child. Her pregnancy proves that was an error all these years." She looked at him, frowning. "Your father may see it that way."

Amir whipped out his cell, texting an answer to Salman, then Umar and Laraib regarding these new developments. Seemed that all of his brothers were in a similar conversation with their wives. "He will not put Kamran on the throne with half breeds as his heirs. What part of this do you not understand?"

"He could easily put him with a second wife—a *Durabian* wife. She can produce those heirs."

His expression went blank as he stared at her bridal garment, torn to shreds under his feet.

"Oh yes, you take my meaning," she taunted. "She has opened a world of possibilities for him. And where will that leave us? And your father has been wavering on a few major issues lately. He could easily appoint Kamran Crown Prince instead of you."

She focused on him, her eyes darting to several areas in the room. "We need to do something that will totally take him out of the running or throw him off center."

"His wife is what makes them vulnerable."

"So, what are we going to do?"

"We kill those half breeds before they can draw breath, and if his wife dies … so be it."

* * *

During the middle of Friday night dinner at the Palace, Kamran stood, moved the plate in front of Ellena and switched his with hers. The spread of Durabian delicacies stretched the length of the main table that seated twenty-four, and the matching tables on either side that was decorated in the same opulent golds and creams—all warm colors.

"Why are you doing that?" Sheikh Aayan asked. "I mean, that is too big of a portion for you, but it is just right for a woman eating for two."

"Or grazing," Eshaal taunted, and Faiza nudged her into silence.

"It is fine," Kamran said, putting his angry glare on Eshaal, who glowered right back at him.

"My son, *why* did you switch the plates?"

That repeated question paused all other conversations at the table.

Kamran locked gazes with his father. "Twice my wife has eaten here and has become extremely ill right after."

"Pregnant women's stomachs can be a little sensitive," the Sheikh said, his tone dismissive.

"It is only sensitive when she comes here," Kamran countered, ignoring the warning look from Ellena. "So, Mama has said tonight I will try what is on Ellena's plate. Next time it will be Mama who will consume what is on her plate. If Ellena does not have any trouble, then it will mean something else entirely."

"It is nothing," Faiza said around a mouthful of rice. "I just had the chef put a little something in it—herbs that helped me when I was pregnant. That is all. I did not realize it upset her so."

"Did you now? All right." Kamran switched his plate with Faiza's and said, "Bon Appetit."

She thrust the plate away, as though it had offended her. "Oh no. I am not pregnant. I do not need—"

He gestured to one of the servants and said, "Please cover this plate and put it in the serving station. And bring me another meal, please."

Faiza breathed an obvious sigh of relief. "Good. All settled."

"What are you going to do with that meal?" Sheikh Aayan asked, peering at Kamal.

"I am taking it to the hospital for analysis."

"Why?" Faiza asked, with wide eyes and a shrill note in her voice.

"If you have to ask, then you are not paying attention." Kamran scanned the faces of those around the table. "My wife will not eat another morsel in this place."

"Just bring her another plate and toss that one in the receptacle," Sheikh growled at the servant.

"Father, you are enabling them to escape the consequences of their actions, ones that specifically show they tried to poison my wife."

"It is not poison," Faiza protested, sharing a worried glance with Eshaal and Hiba, who tried to avert their gazes under their husbands' heated glares.

Kamran left his position and bore down on her. "Then what is it … exactly?"

She shrank back, and didn't respond, but Amir stood, trying to put some space between them.

"That's all right," Kamran said, shrugging. "The lab will tell us. I will have proof."

"It is merely a misunderstanding," Nadeem said, placing a hand on Hiba's shoulder in an obvious attempt to keep his wife quiet.

"A misunderstanding is … putting raisins on a salad when someone doesn't care for it," Kamran countered. "A deliberate act is when someone is allergic to a food item and the host puts that very thing in the meal and doesn't inform the guest. To put something in my wife's food so that it creates stress on her body, so much so that she might lose the child she carries, is attempted murder. All I have to do is prove it."

"Apologize now," Sheikh commanded, eyes flashing fire at Faiza. "End it here."

"More than apologies are required, Father," Kamran said in a voice that brooked no resistance. "If we cannot trust the food that is being given to my wife, then how do you expect us to come here every Friday to break bread?"

"We will switch out her meals with someone at the table each time for you to be sure. Does that work?" Amir said as the Sheikh nodded.

"No, addressing the culprit works." Kamran extended his hand. "Come, Ellena." He maneuvered past the guests until he was by her side. "My issue is what happens when they demand that the chef or the servants do something else. They are not in a position to refuse. Especially if they wish to keep their jobs."

The Sheikh ignored his wife's warning to allow Kamran and Ellena to leave. "Bring the chef."

One of the servants left his station at the head of the table, and ran to do his bidding.

The chef was a round-faced, barrel-bellied man with something akin to a handlebar mustache.

"What did you put in her food?"

He flickered a panicked look at Faiza and Eshaal before focusing on the Sheikh.

"Answer me!"

"I … I … I do not know," he stammered, wringing his pudgy hands.

"Who gave it to you?"

The tense silence was so thick, one could slice it in half.

"Your Highness, I beg you," Chef Zain implored. "They said it would help her indigestion. I do not know what was in that powder."

"Bring the container to me," Kamran demanded.

The chef complied and a few minutes later he ran back with a vial and handed it to Kamran, who held it under his nose and inhaled. "No smell." Then he touched his fingertips to the opening and placed it on the tip of his tongue. "I taste almonds and garlic. I believe this will come back from the analysis as either cyanide or arsenic."

Sheikh Aayan glared at Faiza. "She and the chef will be punished for this devious act."

"And my brother?" Kamran queried, causing several people to gasp.

"Your brother?" The Sheikh frowned as if he heard wrong.

"Yes, you're punishing her, but not him."

Sheikh waved away that thought. "He said she gave it to him."

Kamran held his ground and gritted out. "Chef Zain said *they*."

"That does not mean he had anything to do with it," Sheikh said. "I am more inclined to think that Eshaal and Faiza were involved."

"Where do you think the poison came from?" Kamran shot back. "Neither one of the women have that type of access. But I digress." He extended his hand. "Come Ellena, we will take our leave."

"We have isolated the threat." Sheikh Aayan stood, his expression thunderous.

"In part, but not all. It is safer for my wife not to be in the palace."

Rashid, Waqas, Saba and Saqib all moved in unison to accompany them.

Kamran raised his voice, adding, "Do not forget that I have to answer to her family if anything happens to her."

He let that statement walk across the room and back for a moment.

"You might not take that seriously, but I certainly do," he said over his shoulder. "Some of those men have a dark past. I have no wish to learn how dark it is."

Chapter 27

"You lied to me," Sheikh Zohaib's shout echoed off the columns and every wall in the palace. His thinning hair, and protruding belly made him seem less formidable than the man he was addressing. "I married my precious daughters to lesser men because your son took their innocence."

Sheikh Zohaib had landed in Durabia much earlier than expected, sending the palace into a frenzy to make everything suitable for him and his family to stay a few days.

"Married them properly," Sheikh Aayan, pointed out. "Do not forget that."

"He took their value first."

Kamran called over Saba and Saqib to translate for Ellena so he could now focus on the conversation and the nuances of the exchange. Word had made it around the Muslim world that Kamran was expecting a child and that information put in question how two Arabian wives managed not to produce any offspring for him.

"Remember, you insisted on the annulment each time, then kept asking for the return of the dowry. Even though your daughters, by law, should have remained here. The better question is how is it that your daughters managed to be here with my son for five years each and boré no fruit but somehow ended up married, then pregnant by men they wanted in the first place?"

Zohaib shared a glance with his wife, Zoya and their son, Crown Prince Sajid.

"Did you think I would not find out?" Sheikh Aayan stated and his tone was more accusatory than anything else. "I found it suspect, but had no proof of their deception until now when Ellena Khan is carrying Kamran's child."

Zohaib gestured rudely toward Ellena. "Your proof is that he sired a child with a nonbeliever?" he scoffed. "He could not impregnate a woman of high caliber. That is not proof."

"Bring your daughters before me," Sheikh Aayan commanded. "Let us hear from them what their actions were."

Zohaib waved him off. "They are married and have children. That proves everything."

"Did you bring them as requested?" Sheikh Aayan asked, his eyes laser focused on Zohaib.

"Yes, they are here," he answered, taking in a nod of assent from his wife, Zoya.

"Bring them before me," Sheikh Aayan growled.

Zohaib bridled with anger, fists waving as he growled. "You cannot command me as if I am one of your subjects."

Kamran shared a speaking glance with Ellena. She, too, had said something was amiss with those years of barrenness. He hadn't given it much thought. Unlike how things would normally be done, everyone had been so quick to proclaim his weakness and not what they perceived as the women's failings.

"There is some deception in this issue." Sheikh Aayan narrowed his gaze on his old friend. "We need to get to the bottom of this."

"By accusing my daughters of such blatant treachery? How does that benefit me?"

"The truth benefits everyone," Sheikh Aayan countered. "Bring them in, or I will have my guards do the honors."

"They are in the garden with my servants," Zohaib conceded in a low tone with a wary glanced toward Kamran.

"What will happen if they are somehow the reason that no children were produced during your union?" Ellena asked Kamran, gripping his arm.

He didn't take his gaze off his father. "Let us not speak on that right now."

"Kamran—"

"Ellena, not now, please, love. In private, we will discuss everything. But right now, I really need to focus without having to manage your fears. My love, please."

She clamped down on anything else she had to say. Kamran took her hand, gave it a gentle squeeze, which still didn't reassure her.

Zohaib took note of the exchange between Ellena and Kamran, then asked, "Are you bringing formal charges?"

"This is an informal inquiry. That is all," Kamran stated. "Also, please bring the royal physician and the servants who were designated for them during their stay here. They will be brought in by my personal bodyguards."

"That will take some time."

"We have time," Sheikh Aayan said as Rashid took off. "Dinner is not for two hours yet. In the meantime, everyone will stay here in this room, so no one is giving any information or guiding them to make answers that are not quite true."

At first, no one moved. Then moments later, people formed clusters to discuss what was unfolding.

Twenty minutes afterward, two servants and the royal physician who had retired a few years ago—were standing before Sheikh Aayan, along with Kamran's first two wives.

"There seems to be a little issue surrounding the time Afifa and Naila remained within these walls. Please explain any unusual activity during their time here."

The tallest of the group stepped forward, "They were just like all the others. So their daily routine was simple."

"Thank you. Anything else?" he hedged. "I know it was a long time ago but whatever you can recall would be a good thing."

Ellena took in the haughty posture of the two princesses, but didn't miss the warning glare the more petite of the two sent to the servant whose lips were twitching in an effort not to speak.

"Actually," that particular servant said, leveling a defiant look at Naila. "I thought it a little odd that they both took the special little vitamins."

Both of the princesses stiffened, and so did the doctor, who had remained silent.

"They were in a silver foil packet in a small plastic case."

Ellena gasped. Saba paused and gave her a curious glance. Kamran stroked her hand as a warning to remain silent.

"I knew they were not ill," Israh, Naila's former servant, said. "And when I asked, they said they were vitamins."

"See, nothing out of place." Zohaib exhaled and nodded as if that put an end to things. "Vitamins are not drugs. Case closed."

"Vitamins do not come in silver foil packets or plastic cases such as those," Ellena said, her voice clear across the throne room.

All eyes turned on Ellena and Kamran.

Sheikh Aayan said, "How do you mean?"

"They described it in enough detail that the doctor is well aware of what they are. She should tell you as she carries more weight than I."

"We do not listen to the word of a non-believer," Zohaib snapped. "Be silent, heathen woman."

"First of all," Kamran said, leaving Ellena's side and moving until he was a few feet away from Zohaib. "That is *my wife* you are speaking to, so watch your tone. Second, she made a valid point, that answer is needed so we can have clarity. And I, for one would like to hear what they have to say."

Sheikh Aayan gestured for Kamran to pipe down. "Go on."

"It was round plastic with a soft white bottom and an orange top," the servant said.

Kamran stole a glance at Ellena, who simply nodded.

"Both of them took the same vitamins?"

"Yes, Sheikh Aayan. Both of them," she replied. "Every day at the same time."

"What is the meaning of these questions?" Zohaib growled, impatience in his stance.

Sheikh Aayan's head tilted as he peered at the two sisters. "Do you wish to tell them, or shall I?"

"They said you were a monster," Afifa cried, wringing her hands. "That you would treat us horribly."

Kamran bore down on them. "Did I ever do anything of the kind while you were my wife? Ever?

"No," she whispered. "I simply wanted to go home. They said if we did not give you children, that we would eventually be sent home."

"And leave here having the world believe I was the reason?"

Kamran accused. "All because you wanted to be with someone else? You allowed the world to believe I was … less than able to sire children, all because you did not wish to fulfill the pledge between our families." Kamran's hands clenched and released. "I did not even tell anyone that neither one of you were virgins when our marriage was consummated."

Gasps and shock echoed loudly in voices around the room. The flurry of discord rippled throughout the guests.

"Because I knew your death would be eminent and I did not want that for you despite what our laws dictate" He circled them, took in their fear. "And you care so little for me to be so dense … why would you?"

"Who gave you the pills?" Zohaib looked over to Zoya, who vigorously shook her head. "You did this? You allowed this to happen? You allowed them to bring shame upon our family. To bring disgrace to Nadaum rule.

The physician closed her eyes and came forward. "Someone asked me for the pills."

"I will deal with this accordingly," Zohaib said on a weary note.

"No, we will," Kamran said with a tone of finality.

"Kamran …" Ellena shook her head, her eyes glassy with unshed tears.

"My wife is asking that I show you mercy, when you deserve none," Kamran explained. "First, for the offense of not being pure when coming to the marriage bed. Then by compounding that grave error and disregarding my kindness by participating in such a cold, calculated deception, that I am still affected by it today."

Sheikh Aayan stood and declared, "They will be stripped of their current marriages and children. They will reside here in Durabia. Of course, the dowry will be restored to Durabia first. Twice the amount, as an apology for the injustice done to my son."

Zohaib sighed with resignation. "Thank you for taking them as your wives once again. You have such a compassionate heart."

The two sisters wept and sobbed.

"No, not that compassionate," Kamran admitted. "They will not be my wives. I have no use for women who saw nothing wrong with changing the world's view of me. Who, by their deception, clearly care more for themselves than they do for anyone else."

Zohaib frowned, glaring up at Sheikh Aayan. "So, they will not be his wives? What will they be?"

"Servants."

He was on his feet, roaring, "But they are Royalty!"

"But they are still breathing," Kamran shot back, and those words seemed to take all the life out of the older man.

"And so shall it be," Sheikh Aayan commanded as Kamran reclaimed the space besides Ellena. "Guards, take them to the servants' quarters. I will visit with them to dole out the first of their punishments. Then they will live out their lives as servants until Kamran says otherwise."

"They also said he was a cruel man," Naila chimed in, tears streaming down her face as she held on to her sister.

Sheikh Aayan scanned her face for a moment before asking, "Who?"

"Eshaal, Faiza, and Hiba," she said, gesturing to the women, who shriveled under the sudden scrutiny. "They said if we stayed, he would find a way to murder us and our father could not protect us."

"We did no such thing," Hiba protested, glancing at Faiza. "Forgive me for speaking out of turn. She does not speak the truth."

"Then where did the birth-control pills come from?" Afifa shot back. "I lived here for five years, rarely set foot outside of the palace, and only saw the royal physicians, who were instructed not to provide them for newlywed wives or wives who had not yet conceived children."

"Swear to Allah," Sheikh Aayan commanded, focusing on Eshaal.

"She claimed she had trouble with her menses," Eshaal protested, scanning her husband's stoic face as though expecting his support in the matter. "We were only trying to help."

Sheikh Aayan leveled a stony gaze on her. "You mean, only help yourself to become a queen, yes?"

Ellena felt the tension rippling through Kamran, who kept a tight hold on her hand.

Sheikh Aayan pondered that for several moments. "From this moment on, Faiza, Eshaal, and Hiba are on a provisional watch." His gaze went to Kamran's brothers, who quailed under his glare. "You must make amends—financial amends to your brother—for your wives' offenses."

"How much are you requiring us to give?" Salman asked.

The question, instead of a protest, was telling. Kamran's brothers were well aware of what their wives had done. More than likely, they were complicit as well.

"Everything in your accounts. Every single amount."

"Father," Amir hedged, swallowing hard to contain his shock that matched his brothers', who stood gaping.

Hiba fainted, and Faiza barely caught her in time.

"Everything?" Laraib croaked and his panic-stricken expression matched Umar and Nadeem's.

"Everything. All property. All monies. All sponsorships. All businesses. You will have to begin again."

"This is so unfair," Nadeem yelled. "The wives you forced on us—"

"In your quest to rule," Sheikh Aayan roared back, shutting him down. "You committed a heinous act."

"It was not me," Laraib countered. "It was the wife you arranged for me."

Sheikh Aayan left the throne and swoooped down on him. "And you knew nothing of her actions?"

Laraib's chin lifted to meet his father's gaze head on. "I. Did. Not."

Sheikh Aayan drew himself up to his full height. "Do. Not. Lie. To. Me."

"I did not realize her deception was so low," he said, backing down under the weight of his father's wrath. "I apologize, father. And I apologize to you, my brother."

"Father, I beg you. Do not strip us of everything. We will be commoners," Laraib protested.

"Any request for living expenses will have to be approved by Kamran. Any purchase, any journey, every major decision or activity in your life must now be at Kamran's discretion."

"Why father?" Nadeem cried, holding onto his brothers. "Why penalize us so harshly?"

"Your machination stole his birthright," the Sheikh said, waving a finger at them. "It is only fair that he has everything of yours."

Kamran stepped forward. "Father, I do not wish to have any—"

The Sheikh glared in his direction, ending any other words of refusal.

"Birth control cannot be dispensed to women. So, who was it that procured those pills for Afifa and Naila?" He scanned their faces, and when no answer was forthcoming, he added, "I am grateful to Allah that I have six wives and fifteen other sons to choose as heirs."

Chapter 28

"I would like a word with my daughters before they are taken away," Zohaib said, and his tone and posture were surprisingly humble. Too humble—the direct opposite of the demeanor he'd displayed the entire time.

"Certainly," Sheikh Aayan replied.

Kamran stiffened, released Ellena's hand, and sauntered toward the throne. "No, I do not think it is a good idea for him to be alone with them right now."

Eshaal sighed her impatience. Kamran favored her with a warning look that shut her down.

"Surely, he will allow a father and mother to say farewell to their daughters," Salman said, glaring at Kamran.

"Father, emotions are high right now," Kamran countered. "I say allow everything a moment to settle and then a private audience will be the reward for their compliance."

"As a courtesy from one Sheikh to another," Sheikh Aayan said, focusing on Zoraib. "I am going to override my son's decision."

"It is harmless," Salman said, trying to make an impression on their father since he now stood a chance at being on the throne. "You are being too critical. Shows that you would not make a good king."

Kamran did not dignify that with an answer.

"Father, I will take my leave," Kamran said, gesturing for his guards and assistants to make haste. "Please know that whatever happens is on your hands."

"Such a drama king," Salman taunted with a smirk.

"Mother, Ellena, Zoya," Kamran snapped. "We are leaving—*right now*."

Zoya hesitated, unwilling to make an exit before seeing the outcome and decisions related to her daughters. She tried to pull away, but a whisper from Farah directly in her ear made the older woman flinch, then lose all color in her olive complexion as she swayed on her feet.

"But what about family prayer?" Ellena protested, staying rooted to the spot. "My directive was dinner every Friday as a condition of remaining with you in the Free Zone."

"Now, Ellena," Kamran commanded and guided her forward.

She reluctantly fell into step beside him. "Kamran?"

"Keep going, Ellena." His tone and the grip on her elbow told her Kamran wasn't open to any argument.

Once they cleared the throne room to the outside foyer, she planted her feet. "I'm not moving another muscle until you tell me what's going on."

The guards and assistants all paused, but they, too, wore anxious expressions.

"I do not command you in anything, but right now I am doing so. Move your feet." He hooked his arm under hers and his mother's, who put her free arm around Zoya before he rushed them all forward.

A couple of minutes later, a series of screams and shrieks tore through the air.

Ellena stiffened along with Zoya but did not stop running.

* * *

Kamran glanced in her direction and it took everything within Ellena not to question him. In her heart of hearts, she already knew. She was grateful he sought to spare her, his mother, and the women's mother the core visual of what had happened.

They piled into two separate cars. The drivers cleared the circular driveway and had them moving toward the gate in record time.

The entire trip was made in solemn silence. The moment they cleared the foyer of their new home, Zoya sank into the first chair she could find.

"Mother, please make yourself at home." He waved toward Ellena. "I need a private moment with my wife."

"I understand," she said, embracing him.

"Would you be terribly upset if we missed the palace dinner tonight?" he asked.

She almost crumpled as she put a little distance between them. "No, my heart is hurting for Zoya right now. I will stay with her."

"I will have the chef make a meal of your choosing."

"I love you, my son." She went up on her toes to kiss his cheek. "You always have had more compassion and mercy than anyone I know." She cupped his face in her hands. "And you were always my favorite."

Kamran smiled. "Mother, you say that to all of your children."

She tilted her head, peering at him a moment. "Actually, I do not."

* * *

Ellena paced in front of their bed, her hands flexing in an effort to contain her emotions. One hand went to her belly in a soothing motion as her thoughts went to her child's wellbeing. On a wealth level, they would have no issues.

Kamran had purchased a building that was on the tail end of construction and had them make major adjustments to accommodate Ellena's choices. The place was elaborately decorated in the same fashion as the palace, with shades of rich purples and golds. Nine bedrooms with ensuite bathrooms, a dining room that seated twenty-four, a living room that spanned out into a solarium leading to an Olympic sized pool and an expansive patio the length of the white stone building. She loved the place and the array of flowers planted in the garden that Kamran had designed especially for her. None of this brought her any peace at the moment.

His foot barely made it over the threshold before she rushed to him.

"Kamran—"

He held up one hand for her to wait until the door closed behind him. His face was pale, almost ashen. All of the fight sifted out of her pores seeing how affected he was by the tragic turn of events. She wanted to wrap him in her arms and hold him for a long while. She did, and when he went limp, shoulders lowered in defeat, he pulled away to look in her eyes.

What she saw there hurt her entire heart.

"You knew," she whispered. "You knew he would do that."

"Yes."

"Has that happened before?"

"Not here in Durabia, but it has happened in surrounding countries. In Zoraib's country, Sharia Law is swift and absolute. And you are right, it is not always fair to women. In this case, the level at which they sank to defraud a marriage cannot go without punishment. I believed stripping them of everything was punishment enough. Making them service those who once served them was punishment enough." He rubbed his hands down his face. "Sheikh Zohaib could not live with seeing his daughters reduced to servants in someone else's sheikhdom. The entire Muslim world would be constantly reminded of their transgressions."

Ellena pondered that for a few moments. "Thank you."

"For what?"

"For getting us out of there before he ... killed them. What's going to happen now?"

Kamran pulled her into his arms. "My father will receive the bride price—double, and now additional money for the loss created by their deaths."

She sighed. *Money again. Women translated into property.* "They hurt you."

"Yes." He linked his hands with hers. "Their actions changed the course of my whole life."

"True, and there was sadness because it was unfair to you, but did that require their lives?"

"No, my love," he answered in a barely audible whisper. "I tried to save them."

Ellena pulled in a deep breath, then let it out. "I know."

"My father would not listen."

"I know that, too," she whispered.

"He did not have to let him do that."

She frowned and drew her head back to study Kamran. "He knew?"

"If I knew, everyone in the palace was aware. My brother enjoys these things. It is barbaric. Salman urged my father to believe my request was weakness when it took so much out of me to ask for their release. Especially at a time when I was absorbing the magnitude of what they had done."

Ellena splayed a hand on his chest. "I am so proud of what you tried to do today."

"My words condemned them," he confessed. "In my anger, I said they were unpure."

"That was true, though."

"But I have kept the secret all this time. Why did I share it today when it caused them so much pain?" He braced himself against the physical comfort she provided. "I should have held my tongue. I let emotions get the better of me."

"They called you a monster," Ellena countered, holding him against her body. "All you did was try to show them how untrue that was. No one can fault you for that."

"I fault me for that," he whispered against her hair.

Kamran stayed in her arms several minutes longer before pulling away.

"Come, we need to see about our guests." He stood, extending his hand to her. "Zoya has lost two daughters. And my father's kingdom has lost a bit of its humanity. I am not sure how I can come to terms with either one."

Chapter 29

"Do you realize you are not going to be next in line for the crown if you do not take action?" Nazia warned as she walked toward the window that overlooked the garden. The servants were still clearing the blood from the throne room. Nothing like that had ever taken place in Durabia. Dinner was canceled and everyone dispersed.

"Father did not listen to him," Salman said with a haughty lift of his chin, moving until he was directly behind her. "He listened to me. That is what is important."

Punishments in Durabia were handled with more … diplomacy and nothing quite so inhumane in the presence of everyone, including women. Those measures only happened in some of the more restrictive countries.

"And the people hate him for it. We have not seen a display of something so brutal among Royals. I am telling you now, our daughters will not marry any princes from Zoraib's family."

"What does it matter?" Salman said, weary of the discussion with his wife. "They deserved it. True, it was not the consequence Kamran had in mind. That man is so weak. What reason did he have to spare their lives? A true king upholds the law. Those women were whores and they shamed the house of Nadaum."

"Yes, but now that the truth is out, all it will take is to give Kamran a second wife, a Durabian wife, and he is back in line for the throne. Exactly where your father wants him."

Silence.

His face grew tight and tense as he contemplated the possibility.

"Oh, now you understand," she taunted. "Faiza warned all of us that woman was going to be an issue. You did not listen to me, but you had better listen to me now. Kamran is gaining the hearts of the people. You, they tolerate. Do you know that when a position became open in his house, nearly every servant in the palace asked to join *their* household? Every servant and guard in the palace would rather be employed by Kamran and Ellena than the man who would be Sheikh. We can barely keep a round of servants, guards, or assistants. Think about that," she admonished. "You should have stayed out of that exchange with your father and you would not now be considered as the reason those two women met their demise."

Fairly chastised, he sighed. "I simply thought Kamran was being sensitive. Weak, again."

"He was being compassionate," she snapped. "Because he understood Sheikh Zohaib's true intent. Shows that your brother is very observant and so is his wife. Their work with rescuing women from places like El Zalaam has not gone unnoticed. And the women, the majority of Nationals are leaning more to him, than to you or any of your brothers. Better be glad it is a rulership and not a democracy, because a vote would mean Kamran Ali Khan is next to sit on the throne."

Salman leaned against the window, absorbing what she said. But he held out hope on one thing. "I know Sheikh Zohaib is extremely upset with Ellena," he said. "Her words are what led to their deaths. Not my involvement in the conversation. Everyone was believing the story about Naila and Isray taking vitamins until Ellena opened her mouth. Then the physician had no choice but to confess that they had been taking birth control pills."

"Kamran's words that they were not pure did not help the situation," Faiza said.

Salman nodded his agreement. "For the Muslim World to know that Sheikh Zohaib's daughters and everyone in his female line need to be purity tested brings such shame to his sheikhdom. He will never live that down."

Now men in both families would have to observe the deflowering on the wedding night to witness signs that the woman was a virgin.

"Did you see the look he gave Kamran?" she asked, moving forward until she was in his arms. Shocking because she almost never did such a thing.

"No, I was too busy with the way he was looking at Ellena. Under all the hatred, his desire was evident."

Nazia inched backward, shaking her head. "What? No. No. No. He couldn't possibly want her."

"He can and he does," Salman said with a knowing smile.

"How can you be sure?"

Salman squirmed and quickly averted his gaze.

She moved swiftly until she stood close to him again. He wouldn't meet her eyes but kept his focus on the carpet patterns.

"Salman!" She waited with her arms crossed in front of her.

"We put a camera in their room so we could record their wedding night."

Naiza's eyes widened to the size of saucers as she gasped, "You did not."

"We did."

She perched on the nearest seat, while thinking that over. "Did you ... watch it?"

Several moments passed before he confessed, "I did."

"And?"

Salman exhaled his frustration and lowered himself next to her.

"Oh, come out with it already," she demanded. "Did he have to mount her like a bull with a heifer? "

"Actually, the things they did ... how they ..." He shook his head as a spike of arousal whipped through him. "It was nothing like rutting with a lower-class woman as we expected."

Nazia peered at him, wondering at the sweat pooling on his forehead. "What do you mean?"

"He really loves her. And she loves him," he admitted, seeming amazed by the whole unexpected situation. "It is as though they could not get enough of each other. And the things she could do with her mouth, those lips, and in her throat ... There wasn't a limp qadib in the room. Some of us were embarrassed." Salman had to adjust his pants before his wife witnessed the effect it still had on him. Sometimes he watched it twice a day. He wished they had more but after that night, Kamran and Ellena left for the States then their own mini-palace in the Free Zone. "We visit El Zalaam and those needs are well taken care of ... but watching Kamran with Ellena, Sheikh Zohaib admitted something he probably regrets."

Nazia perked up, then slid to the edge of the chaise. "What?"

"I cannot say." He studied his clasped hands.

"Do not become shy now," she cajoled. "What did he say?"

Salman looked at his wife, torn with indecision. Then he said, "He has not been able to get an erection for years. That's why he stopped taking in new wives."

Nazia mulled that over for a long while. "So, he wants her?"

"Oh yes, he most certainly does."

She smiled and the sight of it was enough to strike a chord of distrust in his heart.

"Then let us make it happen," she said.

Sheikh Aayan might believe that Faiza, Eshaal, and Hiba were the most cunning of women in the palace. Salman would beg to differ. His wife, Nazia, was truly the most deadly, and she, not the other women had actually been the mastermind behind the poisoning. Effectively eliminating the main competition that lay between Salman and the throne. All she did was suggest a certain thing, and the others blindly executed a plan, then carried it out, believing that they alone would sit next to their husbands who took the throne.

"What do you mean?" Salman said, though he was almost afraid to ask.

"Sheikh Zohaib leaves in a few days, maybe sooner. You have the ear of his Crown Prince, Sajid? We have to be smart. Make plans for a year from now. By that time Kamran will let his guard down and forget his statement about not coming to the palace because he's offended. We befriend him, all of us, slowly. Go to their home for dinners."

Salman leaned his back against the window.

"Then we have a celebration for their children's first birthday. Here in the palace. Surprise them, and invite everyone who is anyone in the Muslim world."

"What purpose will that serve?"

"Sheikh Zohaib and his sons will be there," Naiza said, grinning. "So let us make sure Ellena Maharaj Khan goes with him. And those little half breeds too."

"Isn't that an extreme plan?"

She waved one hand in a dismissive way. "Even if it comes to a point that Zohaib returns Ellena to Durabia, no one will believe she was untouched by him or possibly another man. Thereby tainting Kamran again. People will say, he couldn't protect his wife, who would now be soiled."

"How will we accomplish this thing?"

"Between you and Sajid, you will find a way to … get her on that plane. The children, too. Say that she is a gift from the future Sheikh of Durabia. Sajid is not going to turn down a chance to make his father happy. And the Sheikh Zoraib will still want her enough to bed her. For revenge, given what happened to his daughters. That's all we need to discredit Kamran."

"That could cause an issue between our sheikhdom and theirs."

She laughed and shook her head. "Do you see your father going to war over a nonbeliever, a woman, a *Black* woman and an American at that?"

He thought about that for a moment, saw the dangerous beauty of this plan and resigned himself to do his part. "Not at all."

"Umar, Laraib, Amir, and your uncles would be on board to take Kamran down a few notches. His happiness with that woman and his joy in the children they are having were secondary to the fact that their father meets with him on a daily basis to discuss the future of Durabia." She paused, then asked, "But she is really that good in bed?"

Salman nodded, then swallowed hard as his pants tented in his groin area. His wife glanced down and saw the resulting action and said, "Oh yes, that alkaliba has to go."

She stormed out of the suite, leaving him to ponder her anger.

Chapter 30

One year later . . .

"What do you mean no one knows what happened?" Kamran roared, his voice ricocheting off the walls of the throne room. "Not to mention our guards and assistants were blocked from coming in and their phones and weapons were taken by my brother's guards. It cannot be a coincidence that the Sheikh suddenly leaves Durabia unannounced, and my wife and all four of my children are missing."

Salman slammed a hand on Kamran's chest. "Are you accusing Sheikh Zohaib of taking your wife?"

"I am saying that something is amiss," Kamran shot back, shoving away his hand. "And the two incidents are not mutually exclusive."

"Maybe she became weary of being last in line for the throne," Umar taunted, rocking on his heels as he gave Salman a sly smile.

"Or she might be afraid that her neck is the next on the chopping block," Laraib tossed in.

"You think this is funny?" Kamran snapped and all three of them inched back. They were well aware that Kamran had signed documents that stated he would not seek the throne, but would retain all land, sponsorships, and endowments for his bloodline in perpetuity. He had done that to protect his wife and children. "Father, I need you to intervene in this matter."

Standing in front of the throne, Sheikh Aayan shrugged. "Maybe she went with him willingly. It is not unlikely for a woman of her ilk to wish for an … upgrade."

So now they were back to this again? His displeasure toward her work with sex trafficking victims was coming through loud and clear. Ellena had made national news and some of the Muslim community were none too pleased. Something had been brewing ever since Ellena had given birth to quadruplets—two of each gender. Minor complications ensued and bedrest was ordered to combat the issues of preeclampsia and to ensure that the children and Ellena both made it through in good health. He felt some of the family's unease, but after signing a document stating that neither he, nor his children, would seek to have the throne, he thought that would be the end of things.

Now he understood exactly the depths of jealousy that would drive the actions of his brothers.

"And maybe someone in this room saw an opportunity to gain favor with Sheikh Zohaib and rid themselves of a problem at the same time." Kamran directed his comments at his two brothers, whose expressions ranged from stoic to blank.

"Enough of this," Sheikh Ayyaan said, waving Kamran away. "I have other pressing matters."

"Tonight, Father," Kamran said through his teeth, trying to hold on to his anger. "Could it be that you don't see the need to act because you do not approve of her work with the women at her rescue center?"

The Sheikh's eyes flashed with anger. "Careful, my son," he warned. "I realize you are upset. While it is no secret that her work brings attention to an issue that should remain a private matter, I had no hand in her disappearance. You know nonbelievers live by their own creed. That is the risk in having her as your wife."

Kamran despaired that he would have to bring her family in on her disappearance and it could mean the death of some of his own family members. Especially if the Kings and Knights didn't get the right answers. "So, you are not going to look into this matter expeditiously?"

His father squared his shoulders. "I will, when the moment presents itself."

Kamran absorbed that blow. "I see."

"Now, we have other matters to attend to," he said, with a dismissive wave that ended the discussion as he beckoned Salman forward.

"As do I," Kamran said, pivoting, then passing Salman, Laraib, and Umar.

"Where are you going?" his father asked.

Lairab and Umar went still. The entire group focused their attention on Kamran.

"To make a call of my own," Kamran said over his shoulder without breaking his stride. He whipped out his cell and keyed in a message. His guards and assistants stayed on his heels.

"I forbid you to call Zohaib and accuse him of something for which you have no proof," Sheikh Aayan growled.

Kamran turned to face his father. "Oh, *that* is not the call I intend to make."

He reclaimed his place on the throne. "Then pray tell, who are you contacting?"

"I believe the people who had something to do with any unfortunate circumstance which has befallen my wife and children failed to remember one thing. That Ellena Maharaj Khan has family. A great deal of them. She has Kings and Knights. Even the Queens, Princes, and Ladies are formidable."

Sheikh Aayan flinched and Kamran moved in, his gaze landing on Salman and Umar who were holding a side conversation probably related to the current situation.

"There are no consequences." Sheikh Aayan squared his shoulder as though unbothered by that assertion. "This is our land. We are protected from them."

Kamran chuckled, knowing full well that was not the case. "You might believe so, but I have it on good authority that fifty percent of her brothers are trained assassins. And one of the queens as well."

Umar, Laraib, Nadeem, and Salman all shared a worried glance. As they should. The Kings of the Castle were as deadly as they were intelligent.

Kamran moved deeper into the room until he was only three feet from his father. "I want you to remember something else. When you asked who gives this woman, only then did all the Kings, Knights, Queens, Princes and Ladies come into full view." Kamran peered at him a moment, then swept a gaze across the rest of the men in the room. "Tell me, do any of you remember seeing them walk into this room like everyone else?"

The silence was rewarding. Maybe then, they would understand the precarious position they were in.

"Every single one of them is deadly—including the women," Kamran warned. "When they find out she is missing, everyone here had better be prepared for what happens next."

Sheikh Aayan mulled that over for a moment. "Then we simply keep you from contacting them. You will remain in the palace until I look into the matter."

"So, you will hold me prisoner here and I will be unable to leave?"

Salman held out his hand. "Until all of this is sorted out. We do not wish to have any unnecessary problems."

Kamran simply glared at him.

"Your phone," Umar commanded.

Kamran reached into his tunic's pocket, extracted the cell, and passed it to Umar who glanced at the screen and frowned.

"What's the passcode?"

Kamran shrugged.

"Funny." Umar sent another glare Kamran's way.

"Kamran, do not make this difficult," Salman snapped. "Your passcode?"

Instead, Kamran slyly flipped him the bird.

Umar struggled to grip the offending finger, but Kamran landed a series of punches, then others jumped into the fray. His guards fended off his brothers and their team and it took twelve men to restrain Kamran and his staff. Even Saba took down one of Laraib's guards.

While Kamran struggled to loose himself from a cluster of men, Salman grabbed Kamran's index finger and pressed it against the pad to unlock the phone, then searched through the recent messages. Reading the last one, he said, "He sent a message to Daron Kincaid and Alejandro Reyes, saying that Ellena is in danger and that she's been taken out of Durabia and into Nadaum somehow."

"You would send such a thing without actual proof of any wrongdoing?" the Sheikh asked.

Umar glanced up at his father. "This says they are already in route."

"It should take them thirteen hours to get here," Lariab said, giving Umar a sly glance. "Sheikh should have completed any business he has with her. In the meantime, we need to keep Kamran away from any other devices."

Salman glanced down at the screen as a message came through. "What does the Knights are closer mean?"

"I do not know."

"You *do* know," Salman growled as the four men gripped Kamran tighter. "You are just being obstinate."

"Could be," he said with another shrug. Kamran hid a satisfied smile at the sight of their unease.

"Do not make this harder than it has to be." Salman glowered at him.

Kamran lowered his gaze to lock in on his brother. "I. Do. Not. Know."

"Answer them," Amir said snatching the phone from Umar's hand and thrusting it in his face. "And do not do anything foolish."

They loosened his hands enough for him to rub his wrists together, then make an attempt to comply. Both looked over Kamran's shoulder as he typed, still flanked by the other men guarding him on both sides.

The Kings are better.

"What does that mean?" Amir demanded once that text was sent.

"It means that no matter what I type," Kamran answered. "If they don't feel she is safe, then they are going to make an appearance."

Salman gestured to the screen. "So, tell them that she is safe."

Kamran typed *Ellena is safe.*

The response came back. *Show me.*

"Now what do you wish me to type," Kamran taunted, rubbing his wrists together.

Show me now came another response.

"Tell them she's indisposed," Salman commanded as Lairab nodded.

Kamran complied.

The response came, *I don't care if she is butt-ass naked, put her on the phone. If she's safe that shouldn't be a problem.*

"We are not going to fool them," Umar conceded with a weary sigh.

Put El on right now!!! Are our nieces and nephews safe? Show us!

"I'm waiting," Kamran said, staring at Salman.

Another message popped up in a flash. *Never mind, we understand what's going on. We've got your back.*

Kamran grinned and felt the first signs of relief. The whole clan was incredible. Everything he wished his biological brothers could be.

Laraib turned over Kamran's wrists and scanned the tattoos on the other side. "Wait. How did they know you were in trouble, too?"

"What are these for?" Umar demanded, then fixed his gaze on Kamran. "She has one too. You are not supposed to have tattoos. It is against Muslim principles."

"Why would you do such a thing?" Sheikh Aayan growled.

"Answer him," Nadeem demanded.

"Because it was required by her brothers. It ties me to her and them on a spiritual level."

"They are coming," Salman said, alarm in his voice.

As well it should be. Kamran had spent countless hours with each of the Kings and most of the Knights. They were fearless and would stop at nothing when family was involved. Kamran resigned himself to the fact that through their stupidity, his brothers had hastened the end of their lives.

"What are we going to do?" Laraib said with a pointed look at their father.

"This is something more than a simple tattoo, isn't it?" Umar said, narrowing his gaze on Kamran.

"Saba will stay here with me." Nadeem's words alarmed Kamran immediately. His brother had been after Saba ever since she had been in the palace's employ.

"If any harm comes to her, you will pay," he warned Nadeem, whose lips curled into a snarl. "Well, while you all sort things out, I am going to sit right here until my new brothers return with my wife."

An evil light shone from Salman's eyes. "What makes you think she will return?"

"I do not have to think." Kamran leveled a stony gaze at him as he sat and folded his legs on the carpet. "I *know*."

Chapter 31

"Why am I here?" Ellena demanded, trying to quell the headache
that greeted her when she opened her eyes to an elaborately decorated
room of reds, golds, and greens. The décor was unlike anything she
remembered. The scent, and even the vibe, meant she wasn't in the
Durabian palace.

Last thing she was aware of was the new driver taking her and the
children to a birthday celebration at the palace. The first visit since
the night that Zoraib's daughters were killed. As she left the vehicle, a
prick of pain on her neck was the precursor to an instant overwhelming
nausea. Then she knew nothing else.

Pain exploded from every side of her face.

"You do not speak unless we ask."

Her hand went up to her cheek, and she sat up, trying to quiet the
ringing in her ears caused by the sudden blow. She glared at Sajid from
where they settled her on the bed.

"Lower your eyes, alkaliba," Sajid snarled. "Do not dare look me in the eyes, as if you are equal to me." He tightened her bindings. "You will be taught the proper way to serve a man. They gave you far too many freedoms in Durabia. You will have no such things here. You will be taught how to properly serve my father. And you had better hope, for your sake, that you become his favorite."

"I have a husband."

"You *had* a husband," he shot back, grinning. "You are in Nadaum. You are Zoraib's now, and for any of his sons to use for their pleasure. No one can get to you."

"My children," she said, her heart slamming in her chest. "Where are my children?"

"Those mongrels," he spat. "They are safe. How well they are treated is up to you." He gave her a disdainful onceover. "My father ... desires you for some reason. You are going to be completely prepared to receive him—and then his sons, after he has had his fill of you."

"I will not submit to any man but my husband."

"Your daughters are ... one year old?" He grinned. "Do you know how much they will fetch on the slave market?"

Fear like she'd never known gripped her. Her breathing hitched and she nearly blacked out.

"Yes. You understand," he said, grinning. "Your children will be safe so long as you do as you are commanded."

"So, you would steal another man's wife and children?"

"We didn't have to steal you," he replied with a harsh laugh. "Salman *gave* you to us. My father is sufficiently impressed by the way you are with Kamran Ali Khan. In time, you will crave his affections. Your life depends on it. The life of your children are in the balance because of it. Are we clear?"

She willed the tears not to fall. They would solve nothing. Neither would giving in to despair. Dro Reyes and Kamran had taught her well. Calm under pressure. Use your mind to fight your way out. "Yes."

"Oh, and if you get it in your head to somehow free yourself by causing my father's death, I will personally make those little mongrels suffer horribly. Maybe have someone …well, you know … take them in that manner and you will have to watch. The fact that they have royal blood, and some are angry that my sisters were killed, only sweetens them. There are men who love that sort of monstrous thing. Are we clear?"

The unbearable picture stole the breath and the fight right out of her, for the moment. "Yes."

"I am sending Latifah to educate you on how to address the Sheikh. I doubt they took the time to train you. You will learn—and fast, for your children's sake."

Sajid left the bed and made it only as far as the threshold, when she spat, "My husband will come for me. My brothers will come for me. If anything, if any harm comes to me or my children, you will not live out your days in peace."

His laughter unsettled her soul. "Oh, you worthless, deluded whore," he snarled. "They do not know where you are. They will never find you."

Ellena felt one ray of hope and she latched onto it with all of her might as she rubbed her wrists together. She focused squarely on him and said, "Trust me, they will."

Chapter 32

"Are we really jumping from a plane?" Shaz asked, peering out of the small window with a lighted grid of cities underneath.

"We need to strike quickly and this is our best play." Daron glanced at his watch, then up at Jai, along with the other Kings and the rest of Dro's men. "Technically, you'll be launched out in about an hour."

They had left the United States to assist Kamran and Ellena the minute they received that first text. They paused only a brief moment when *Ellena is safe* came through, but knew something was extremely wrong when Kamran's tattoo signaled that he was also in trouble.

First, they only had a general location for Ellena to go by—and then her signal came. Dro lowered his head into his hands. Daron rubbed his shoulder, saying, "Our safety precautions have served us well. We knew her disappearance might be a possibility one day. At least, we spent that time showing her how to use various weapons."

"You have a point. But killing is not in her nature." Dro let out a heavy breath. "One hesitation could cost her life. You know that."

"You'd be amazed at what a mother will do to protect her children," Daron told him.

"Think about Camila," Shaz said with a tilt of his head, meaning the woman he loved who almost took the head off a dirty politician who was using underhanded methods to get his hands on her child.

They had been in the air for almost half a day after spending eight hours scrambling to get a strategy in place and gathering the equipment to pull off a rescue in the heartland of Nadaum.

"I was just confirming we're going with that plan," Shaz said, peering over Daron's shoulder.

Jai stood and walked to the center lower level of the hybrid plane.

The upper level where they'd been sleeping had the decor of a luxury jet. The lower level was the no-frills, nuts and bolts segment of the plane with cargo boxes, equipment, and an information console set up in the center.

"Nicco is jumping first. If you want to jump in tandem with him instead of using The Arabian, let me know." Daron watched as Cameron, Mia—the partner of the inventor of the personal cloaking device they would use, and Nicco—one of the ex-military men who was his right hand—worked at setting up a hovercraft contraption—The Arabian—for the launch. The hovercrafts, which looked a cross between a jet ski and a motorcycle, were specifically outfitted to ensure the Kings landed safely on the ground. All were equipped with a manual and remote function. The biggest issue with their mission was that Kamran and Ellena were in two separate places with more than an eleven-hour driving distance between them. He'd thought Cameron was crazy when she suggested the jump into Durabia on the way to Naduam but one thing his woman did well was planning and execution. The flight time between sites was just under two hours and coming up with a two-pronged attack was genius.

One team was headed to Durabia, where Kamran was being held hostage and another team to Nadaum to extract Ellena and the little ones. The plane would make a sweep through Durabia then land at a strip of land extremely close to the palace in Nadaum. Once Ellena and the children were recovered, they could quickly fly back to Durabia to help with executing the Knight's part of the plan to deal with Kamran's predicament. He was on home base and things were a lot more precarious because family was involved. That's why Dro had brought Marena, a biochemical weapons expert and scientist, and Alexa, one of the guardian elite team, in on the Durabia part of the operation.

"Nicco, pull up the Durabian palace. Let's do a quick review." Daron moved to the table set up in the center of a stack of metal cargo boxes. Nicco displayed a hologram. "Hiram and several other Knights will pick Team One up from the designated location in the dunes."

Vikkas and the remaining Kings joined Jai and Daron at the console.

"We need to get into these cities undetected with our equipment and minimum interference. The Arabians will allow us to do this." Daron nodded to the advanced hovercrafts that sat near the airplane's hatch.

"We're still going with a two-pronged attack?" Vikkas asked, sliding into a dark, hooded jacket.

"Yes. Team One is already headed to the location the Knights have deemed the best and safest point. Then Team Two will be dropped at another location in Nadaum." Daron held up two fingers, indicating that Nicco should display both locations side by side. "Having a few of the Knights already in the Free Zone, because they had started businesses with Kamran, was a blessing. Khalil is flying commercial along with two of the Knights to throw them off."

"We need to pack the gear in the trucks quickly and head to the palace," Vikkas added.

"The Knights will bring you to the entrance." Daron laid his index finger on the holograph where they were to enter, then shifted it to the green dot where Kamran was being held. "This is where you're heading once inside."

"You won't move in until Team Two confirms that we have Ellena and are headed back your way," Shaz reminded them. "Unless Kamran's situation requires immediate extraction. He knows to send another signal if that becomes the case."

"Where are Dwayne, Jai, and I setting up the command center?" Grant cleared the table and stepped closer, his solemn expression mirroring the strain the others were under. So many elements to pull together in an impossible amount of time.

"You'll be a quarter of a mile out." Daron glanced at Cameron and Mia as they packed the storage containers on the back of the Arabians then studied the tablet to see how far they were off their target. "Nicco will release the drones first. Once they're in position, your mobile command team will be up and running to be their eyes inside."

"Once we reach Kamran?" Reno questioned.

"It'll be a judgment call," Dro answered.

Daron picked up the clear square called "the wall" which was a shield. Once it hit the ground, the device extended seven feet in height and quadrupled in width. "You can each link up the wall shield for extra safety before releasing Kamran."

"But they can't see us with the Emperor's suit." Kaleb frowned and looked first to Reno then Daron, referring to the technology created by Calvin Atwood which camouflaged the wearer by making them appear invisible to the naked eye. When the Suit was turned on, it projected the images around the user to blend into the surroundings.

"We don't know how they're restraining Kamran or what they're using to keep him in check," Daron replied, returning the device to the table. "If they're shooting near Kamran to invoke fear, one of you could get hit."

"What if we don't need the wall shield?" Vikkas asked.

"Then assess any injuries and gear Kamran up with a gun and personal shield." Daron watched as Nicco walked over and strapped on the parachute.

"Kamran will be calling the shots from there, correct?" Dwayne asked as he took one of the face masks and goggles that Mia was handing out to the Kings.

"Yes, the next move is his to make." Daron pulled up the controls for The Arabians. "We're there to keep him safe while he executes his plan."

"It's time," Cameron announced as she closed the lid on the storage unit and prepared to ride.

Chapter 33

"Father, she is only partially prepared for you," Sajid protested, his frustration evident in the tight set of his shoulders.

"Delightful. Exquisite skin," Sheikh Zohaib said, stroking Ellena's bare shoulders and ignoring his son's warning. "You know, my first was an African slave girl. My father believed we should slake our lust on those who are inferior. He said we should treat the Arabian girls with a touch more … patience and care." He closed his eyes. "Africans were our only choice. Their screams were delicious. The blood. So much blood. Made me thirsty for others. He bought them pure, right before they flowered." He kissed Ellena's shoulder, tasting her skin.

She shuddered as he continued speaking. "Waiting for that precious sign was torture. But oh, when they did … to be the first to break them, to tear through that thin membrane of flesh. To watch the pain extinguish all form of hope in their eyes. Witness when they reached the understanding that they were powerless to do anything to stop what was being done to them. That this was now their life—to be at the mercy of men. That is a beautiful thing to behold."

He lifted her chin so she met his eyes. "I watched you with him. I have never seen anything so magnificent."

"Father," Sajid began another warning as Ellena stared at him, horrified.

"What difference does it make if she knows they were recorded," Zohaib snapped, glaring at his son. "She will not see her beloved Kamran ever again. And she will do everything in her power to protect her children. So, she's going to be a good slave. Powerless to do anything but what I desire." Zohaib grinned and the sight of it spiked Ellena's heart rate. "I will have you for as long as you please me." He leaned in, pressed a kiss her lips. She whimpered with the effort it took to hold back her revulsion.

"That sound." He laughed. "Like a wounded animal. Such a pleasure. See what it does to me." He guided her hand to his erection, and she froze. She flickered a gaze to Sajid, whose expression was dark and forbidding.

"Oh, she worries that we will have eyes on us as she submits to me." Zohaib waved his son away. "Leave us."

"Father—"

"Leave us," he commanded more forcefully. "What can she do? You hold the life of her children in your hand. She will be good for me. Make me a believer—or she will watch as they are violated before they die."

Ellena gripped the bed covering, trying to center herself before she passed out.

"Yes," he said on a breathy whisper. "That light of hope has diminished. It was there a minute ago. Now it is … poof." He glared at his son, who still remained despite Zoraib's wish.

Sajid trudged away, closing the door behind him.

"This is now your life. Kamran Ali Khan will not come for you. His father will not allow it. And you are not worth it. For him to pursue you is an act of war."

"And stealing me was not?" She shot back, startling him.

"Stolen! You were a gift from the future king," Zohaib said with a salacious grin.

"A gift he was not sanctioned to give."

"Semantics. There will be no one who cares enough about a woman like you to incite a war. You are deluded about your own importance."

"Just as you were deluded and outsmarted by your daughters," Ellena countered.

Pain blinded her for several moments from the blow that landed on the side of her head.

The door swung open and Sajid rushed in. "Father, I heard."

"Did I not say to leave us?" Zohaib roared.

Sajid gave a slight bow but flickered a gaze at Ellena, who held a hand to her head. "Yes, Father."

"Do not interrupt us again," Zohaib growled. "Why are you so worried? She is firmly under our control."

"But does she know what that means, Father? She is heathen and wild. American women feel that rules do not apply to them."

"I thought you said she had been prepared for me?"

"She is, physically, but she has not been broken mentally, yet. You were too impatient to have her and I wasn't done."

"Then you are not the son I raised. Letting a woman—an African woman get the better of you."

"She is not African," Sajid shot back. "She is American born."

"She is inferior." He dismissed him with a flick of the wrist. "Leave us, and I will not tell you again." He turned a lascivious gaze on Ellena. "Now, where were we? Ah, yes, that precious thing that you do with your mouth ...."

Chapter 34

Without hesitation, Nicco jumped from the side door of the plane as Jai, Grant, Vikkas, Dwayne, Reno, and Kaleb walked over to The Arabians.

"Cameron, Mia, and I will be in control of The Arabians until you reach the mode where you're hovering only a few feet off the ground. At that point, Nicco takes over the control and shifts the device to ground mode."

A blur of activity ensued upon his command.

"Seeing this is our first time going out of a plane on them, we're fine with that." Vikkas slid onto The Arabian.

"It's very important to maintain your locked-in position until you reach the ground and a few yards from our target," Daron reminded them as he neared the hatch where the Kings were getting on their assigned Arabians. "Small movements are all right. Sudden, large ones will be problematic."

"Very comforting." Jai slid the goggles over his eyes.

Kaleb buckled himself in, clicked his feet into the mechanism, then pulled out the armrest and slid in his limbs before engaging the safety.

"Everyone locked in?" Daron maneuvered around the men doing a quick check-in, wishing they had time for some dry runs before this actual moment. Time wasn't something they had in spades.

"Yes," the men replied in unison.

Daron and the remaining team moved to a secured station as the hatch inched open and the warm night air entered the aircraft. Jai and Vikkas were launched under Cameron's control. The hovercraft lifted from the plane's metal floor and glided into the night sky. Mia guided Reno and Dwayne out next.

Grant and Kaleb were last out, under Daron's control. The hatch slowly closed. Grant and Kaleb's Arabians descended smoothly. Daron's heart raced as he watched Kaleb's Arabian suddenly spin counterclockwise on the screen. He fought to regain control, moving Grant farther away so Kaleb wouldn't crash into him.

"Kaleb, what's going on?" Daron knew he was still wavering since the unit wasn't back under control.

"My hand slipped and I accidentally released the arm locks," Kaleb's voice held a tinge of panic. This far up, he could be severely injured. They were all well aware of the risks.

"Damn," Daron muttered, knowing that remotely relocking the arm unit could injure Kaleb if he wasn't in the right position. "Breathe. Slowly return your body to its original pose. You'll be fine even without the arm safety engaged."

The unit finally stopped spinning.

"He's probably feeling nauseous right now." Cameron leaned in, scanning Daron's control unit.

"True, but he's still on the machine and alive." Daron sighed with relief as the thumping of his heart slowed when the two Arabians units' controls were finally taken over by Nicco.

The team to retrieve Ellena was smaller because they were going into the situation without much intel. Besides Shaz, the individuals on Team Two had more hands-on experience in dealing with similar circumstances.

Daron headed to where Dro and Shaz were gearing up to make the jump. Cameron held out a hand with his equipment.

"See you down there." Cameron winked at him then jumped from the plane, followed by Mia.

"Maybe I should have left with Team One." Shaz swallowed hard, then paused at the open door.

"Too late now." Dro gave him a push then followed him out.

Daron made the jump into the darkness. The face mask almost suffocated him as the air forced it back on his face. If he didn't have it on when he hit the ground, he'd be choking on a mouthful of sand. One thing that made him uncomfortable was not being able to see those clear parachutes deploy in the darkness. If it had been daylight, there would have been a little ripple of rainbow color catching the clear material. The fact that no one seemed to be panicking was his only relief. He didn't need anyone getting tangled up because they didn't know to shift to avoid someone's parachute. He made a mental note to place something on the material to make it detectable at night. If they had cause to use them again.

The team took a greater risk to land them in an area extremely close to the palace rather than farther out to make their way on foot. When he hit the ground, the sand flew up as Daron slightly overshot his landing zone. Cameron and the team rushed forward, gathering up the parachutes. Falcon and a few other Knights' trucks headed toward them in the distance.

Now came the hard part—getting Ellena and the children out and getting to Kamran in Durabia without fatalities on their side.

Chapter 35

Ellena drew on every ounce of strength she could summon. She had to fall back on all levels of training, thinking of a way to escape. No gun in sight, so hand to hand would be her best option.

While in the Nation, she was tasked to be under Sister Aisha as a Vanguard—the elite group of women who were security to the Minister and other upper ranking members of the Nation. She only made it through because of the encouragement of the sisters, not necessarily on her own steam. Ellena was not the right size for a Vanguard, but they allowed her into the program anyway, believing she would lose the excess pounds during martial arts, drills and extreme fitness maneuvers. She did, but not enough to become a valued part of a special security detail.

Many women dropped out along the way—women who were the perfect size for Vanguard requirements. But she made it all the way to the end—at her size, only a little smaller than Ellena was at the moment. So many times, she wanted to give up, but their encouragement kept her going. Every single time. She had amazed everyone and even herself.

Ellena calmed her mind and realized that at one point Zohaib would be vulnerable. She had to do whatever it took to save herself and her children. Dro had told her once that what he loved most about the Queens of The Castle, was that they waited for no one to save them. They learned to defend themselves and accept help only when warranted. She was a Queen in her own right.

She waited for Zohaib to lean back on the bed, believing by her defeated posture she would totally submit to his demand. Moments later, when he closed his eyes, she did two things at once. Ellena pushed the sheet toward his mouth and clamped down on his delicate flesh. Her teeth sliced through the first layer of his skin as she pressed the cloth into his mouth and pushed his chest to anchor him to the mattress. She bit down harder, tearing through more flesh, and then with all of her might she yanked away, separating his erection from the rest of his body.

Ellena recovered quickly from the effort it took and spat the coppery taste from her mouth. She shifted on the bed to avoid the blood spray as she moved toward his chest, forcing more of the cloth into his mouth, to muffle his screams. She covered his grunts and attempts to escape from her with loud, sensual moans that elicited hoots of laughter from those on the other side of the door.

"The old man still has it," Sajid said, chuckling. "Come, let us get a drink."

She pressed down hard on the material at his groin to staunch the flow. If he died, all would be lost. As his body thrashed, she ran to the credenza, grabbed the ice from the gold bucket, then packed it on his groin as tightly as she could.

Zohaib's anger flowed into panic before his eyes fluttered and closed. She picked up that delicate piece of flesh and some of the ice, sliced off a section of the shower curtain and wrapped both before opening the toilet's tank and dropping it inside.

She cleared the blood from her face, while trying to steady her trembling hands. She dressed quickly in his clothes then opened the door to find the two guards chatting.

Ellena lowered the timbre of her voice, gruffly asking in Arabic, "Where are the children?"

They each turned toward the door and pointed eastward.

"Take me."

One of the guards frowned and peered at Ellena. He moved forward at the exact moment she opened the door all the way, snatched the gun from the holster of the man who stood closer to her, and pointed it at the advancing guard.

"You cannot—"

One shot to his temple ended that conversation.

"Would you like to join him?"

The remaining guard held up his hands and shook his head.

"Take me to my children."

"You will never make it past the others," he said as she extracted the gun from the fallen guard and tucked it safely into the belt of the tunic.

"You'd better hope that I do," she warned. "You'll die before I will."

They traveled down the dimly-lit hall. Along the way, she took out several more unsuspecting guards.

"You only have one more bullet left in that gun," the guard said over his shoulder.

"Thanks for the reminder." She ditched that gun and aimed at his back with the other, then scooped one more weapon from one of the guards on the floor.

"Walk."

"You know they're going to kill you," he warned.

"Not if I kill them first."

She put a bullet in another guard before moving forward. The man in front of her shook and went quiet.

"What's your name?" She prodded him in the back.

His voice quaked as he said, "Ridwan."

"Well, Ridwan, we are getting my children and I am leaving and going back to my husband. If anyone tries to stop me, let them know that Sheikh is missing a vital piece of ... equipment. And if they want a chance to reattach it, they will let me pass."

His head swiveled and he turned wide eyes on her. He had lost every ounce of color in his face as her true meaning hit. "That is ... horrific."

"Yes, but so is stealing a woman and her children," Ellena shot back. "I don't give a damn about anything but getting what's mine and getting gone."

"You ... you ... you." He shivered and went quiet.

"Yes, yes, yes," she said in a weary tone as she followed him past another set of rooms. "I separated the king from an important part of his body."

The guard spun to face her. "What you have done is punishable by your death. He cannot be buried without all of his ..." He inhaled. "They will never let you live behind something so ... despicable."

"Well, he should have thought about that before trying to put it where it didn't belong, and wasn't wanted. I am Kamran Ali Khan's wife and I am not here by choice. Now move!"

He gestured to the door at the far end of the hall, then knocked. When he received permission, he turned the knob and pushed it open. The spacious room was illuminated by bright lights and even brighter colors.

"Mama!" Her babies toddled to her, laughing.

The women looking after them backed away at the sight of the weapon.

"You," Ellena gestured to a woman with auburn hair, a white tunic, and almond-shaped eyes. "Pick up my son. You ..." she pointed to another woman in similar dress. "Pick up my daughter and come here."

When the women shuffled forward, she leaned in to whisper to her children. "I need you to be very quiet, okay?" Then she directed two other women to pick up the remaining two after she kissed them.

They bobbed their heads, their eyes wide with shock but they stopped reaching for her and held onto their nurses. The caravan of children, nurses, and one guard swiftly covered the ground past a few open areas before the guard said, "You're not going to want to go that way."

"Why?"

"It will lead to the side entrance to the garden and out the back way to the road."

"I feel cool air coming from that way," she said. "That's the exit."

"Yes, but—"

"Why should I trust you?" she snapped, poking him with the gun once more. "Move."

They went forward, silently covering several yards to the door, only stopping for one reason.

"Where the hell do you think you're going?"

Chapter 36

Ellena looked with longing at the exit behind Sajid.

"Your father is going to be minus a particular body part if you don't get out of my way," she warned Sajid, brandishing the weapon in his direction.

"I cannot let you leave."

"The longer you wait, the less likely it will be that the surgeons can reattach it. Your call."

Only then did Sajid's eyes widen and the panic set in as he commanded the guards with him, "Search his room."

"You won't find it in time," she said, smiling. "You can let me walk out of here, with my children, and I'll tell you when we make it to a safe point. Or your father will become known as a King without a Kong."

One of the nurses grimaced. The other tried to hold back a smirk.

Sajid growled and shook his head. "You will not make it out of Nadaum alive."

"We beg to differ."

All focus turned to the group of men storming through the door dressed in all black and carrying an array of weapons.

Ellena was never so happy to see her family in her entire life. "You came for us."

"Damn straight."

Ellena fell into Dro's arms as the Kings fanned out, each taking one of her children in their arms.

"How did you get in here?" Sajid demanded, watching as his brother Noman was pushed into the enclosed space.

"We did not see them coming," one of the guards protested as Shaz walked in behind him.

"Never mind all that," Dro said, shifting warily until he stood in front of Ellena. "El, I'll take this."

Her hands trembled so badly, she couldn't hold the gun straight. "I had to—"

"I know, El. I know," he said with a reassuring whisper.

"Where is Kamran?" she asked as her heartbeat pounded in her ear.

"They're holding him hostage at the palace," Daron said. "From what the Knights told us, they had to restrain him because he was about to wage a full-blown war for your return. But then he called in his brothers."

Daron reached for her hand and stroked the tattoo with his index finger.

"Thank God, you insisted," she said of the tattoo that Hiram had place there and the matching one on Kamran.

"Come, let's get out of here before they do something stupid." His attention went to Sajid. "You're coming with us."

He stepped back. "I must stay and see to my father's health."

"He has other sons for that," Shaz said.

Sajid planted his feet. "But if they attend to him, they will be the next in line if something happens."

"That sounds like King boy problems to me," Vikkas taunted. "Not my circus. We have to go."

"They will need to come with us," Ellena said, gesturing to the women and the one guard who'd been with her throughout the entire ordeal.

"El, we don't have room—"

"They will be killed," she warned. "Especially him. He could've taken me out twice before I made it here, because I'm not real good at this."

Daron shook his head. "All right everybody. Let's move."

"Where are you?" Shaz spoke into the com device.

"We're headed your way," Nicco responded. "Might need another chopper. We've got company."

"How many extras?"

Daron scanned the group a second time. "Six."

"We can handle it. Get your asses in gear. We're about to have the wrong kind of company."

As they moved toward the exit and certain freedom, Sajid yelled, "Wait! You did not tell them where my father's ..." He swallowed hard. "...qadib is."

Ellena glanced over her shoulder, looked him square in the eye and said, "I didn't. Did I?"

Chapter 37

"Barbaric," Kamran said and that one word echoed off of every wall in the palace. "Your actions are of a barbaric nature. So fearful of losing status, of losing power, that you committed such atrocities against my wife and would visit horrific pain on my children. Do you know they were going to sell them to slavers and planned to violate them in ways you could not imagine." He sighed and his shoulders drooped. "My brothers had nothing to fear from me. Nothing whatsoever, but they saw Ellena, and my precious children as so much of a threat, they allowed Sijad to take them, and you supported it by your inaction. Simply to rid yourselves of a problem."

Kamran paced in front of the Kings. "I will say this, and I do so openly. Here is my right hand to Allah." He raised his arm. "Besides my mother and sisters, if I see one family member's face come towards me, my wife or my children, I will shoot first and ask questions never."

When his chest stopped heaving, he snatched off his head covering and ran one hand through his hair, ruffling the dark strands.

"There was no reason to do what you did," he said, sweeping a gaze across all of them. "I had already signed documents that meant neither I, nor my children, would have any interest in or claim to the throne. You all knew and yet you still came for us."

He watched his brothers avoid his gaze before he continued, "We claim to be better than Americans but we are no better. Their current leadership and the people who follow him have this same greedy, divisive mentality. We claim to be better than Christians, yet we are no better. They are so fearful of people who look like us, who look like Ellena, that they enact laws to ensure they can never reach their full potential without nearly three times the obstacles others face. They, like us, treat women, as inferior. So, do not ever work your lips around the words that we are better than anyone.

"The difference between us and them is oil. The difference is the source of our money. But the truth of the matter is that the source of our evil is the same. This does not bring us closer to God. These actions that put my wife on Nadaum soil were prideful, and not in the spirit of peace. Barbaric natures can be traced back to the foundation of almost any culture, but we are supposed to be civilized and an example of the best Allah has to offer. The *best* example."

He swept an eagle-eyed gaze across his brothers, all of whom stood together in solidarity with each other. "I leave this place with burdens so heavy that it will take the rest of my life to lift. But here is where you made a mistake. You failed to remember our wedding day. You failed to remember her family—the Kings, the Knights, the Queens. They are all on their way here. They came for justice. And they will not be denied.

"The moment I leave the place and step outside, all manner of hell is coming your way. The only persons I am inclined to protect are my mother and sisters, who are already outside of the palace shopping, I believe, with the rest of the women and children." A sinister smile twisted his lips. "I made sure they left the grounds this morning. My brothers and their wives who are still here—all of you can burn in hell. Better yet, maybe having you lose something important, maybe being at the mercy of others will be just the lesson you need. "

"If your exit is when *hell* starts, then all we have to do is make sure you do not leave," Salman said as their father grimaced.

His brothers Umar and Nadeem closed in.

"Father, is this truly something you wish?" Kamran asked, beyond feeling surprised at this point.

"Kamran, I am truly sorry that it has come to this," he said, frowning as he watched Marina and Alexa going from his guards, assistants administering some type of clear liquid into their eyes. "If it means my life, the life of my sons, and safety of the sheikhdom, then you must remain here for a time."

Salman gestured toward his personal guards. "Take them to the lower quarters."

Alejandro Reyes suddenly flickered into view, standing next to Kamran. After a flash of light, Daron was in full view. Soon, all nine Kings, all nine Knights, Cameron, Mia, Alexa, Grayson, and Nicco stood around the room.

Sheikh Aayan shook his head as his grip tightened on the hand rest. "How ... how is this possible?"

"I warned you that her family would not stand for her to be mistreated." The Knights and the Kings disappeared again. Seconds later, they appeared. One stood next to the Sheikh and the rest surrounded other members of the Royal Family.

"As I said before, her family has her covered." Kamran folded his arms and wore a satisfied smile.

Ellena came through the doors, and the sight of her hurt his whole heart. Though she tried to hide her emotions behind a smile, he could tell she had been through hell. Her eyes were tired and she wore men's clothing—a sheikh's clothing. And the bloodstains were evident. His or hers?

Even with all that, her air was triumphant. He wondered, only briefly, about the children's whereabouts. Then surmised that if she was here, and her brothers had been successful in their mission, then the children were safe.

He would never fail her again. Would never become so comfortable around people that he would believe they weren't capable of taking drastic action to maintain power and status.

"Oh, and just so you know," Kamran said to his father. "They consider me family too."

With that, he turned toward Marina and took the vial from her hand.

"My son," the Sheikh cried out as he stood. "Have mercy on us all."

"You had no mercy on my wife," Kamran roared.

"You could have another wife," Aayan roared back. "An *Arabian* wife, with Arabian children."

"And now the real Sheikh comes out." Kamran kissed the back of Ellena's hand. "This woman is the only wife I desire. I have no need of anyone else." He held the vial in the air. "This is your consequence. This is your punishment. This will render you temporarily sightless. Everyone here who has not been given the treatment that Marina has graciously given the rest of us, will be blind."

"Blind?" Sheikh Aayan croaked.

"Yes, for a short period of time. I have already informed your friend, Sheikh Zoraib that you wish an audience with him regarding the matter with Ellena. Whenever he recovers from his surgery, imagine what he will find when his men usher him into the palace. This time next week, Durabia will be under Nadaumian rule. Do you believe your good friend—one you were only too willing to sacrifice my wife to his prurient desires—will return the favor by giving your kingdom back to you when you resurface? I think not."

Sheikh Aayan's jaw hung open. "You would leave us vulnerable to him this way?"

"It's better than leaving you dead."

"My son—"

"Do not call me that," Kamran snapped. "Ever."

"Why would you not take the kingdom for yourself?" he squawked, his arms outstretched. "I will … I will relinquish my crown."

"Father." Salman stepped forward. "Do not do this. Let me have the crown. I will do away with him and all of these non-believers. We still have control of the assets, everything."

"It is too late for that," Kamran said, and the thought filled him with sadness. The chemicals were already seeping in from the air vents.

"I am leaving. This place will be too much for my wife and children to endure."

"Then appoint someone," Aayan pleaded. "But please do not leave us so vulnerable that we lose everything, this palace, our homes—all of it."

"Appoint someone?" Kamran's bland expression gave no clue to his thoughts.

"Father, I beg of you do not do this," Umar croaked, until Aayan shut him down with a gesture.

"Kamran, leave someone in your stead," Aayan commanded, ignoring all of the panicked expressions and utterances from his other sons. He stepped down from the platform. "My word to Allah that the one you choose will receive all access to everything needed to run the kingdom until you see fit to restore it under your rule."

Ellena met Kamran's eyes, then smiled as she lowered her gaze to their joined hands. Her gaze slid to the empty space on his right.

Kamran looked at her for a moment to ascertain the message she was trying to get across to him. Then she reached out, stroking a whisper soft touch on what seemed to be nothing but air. He smiled as it dawned on him, and o he said, "Very well. I choose … Khalil Germaine Maharaj."

Everyone gasped. Sheikh Aayan turned several shades of red, then the palette went in the totally opposite direction and he went pale. A Maharaj—an East Indian line of Maharaj on the throne was sacrilege!

Khalil slowly became visible to everyone in the room. "Have you lost your mind? I was pushed out of my family for not wanting this very thing. This unhealthy competition with his father and mine. Cost me years with my wife and children."

Kamran said, "You wish to make a difference in the world. Start here, where you can be the most impactful. Do not talk about it, *be* about it."

Even the Kings grimaced at that one.

"He does have a point," Hiram said, grinning.

Khalil's expression was nothing short of stunned. "Who have you been hanging around?"

"One guess." He glanced over his shoulder at the Kings, then his gaze slid to his own biological brothers. "Salman, Amir, Laraib, Nadeem, Umar, my uncles, and their wives must pay for the crimes committed against my wife." A sneer lifted Kamran's lips. "Personally, losing their sight permanently would be fair and just, leaving them to rely on others for everything. That is fitting." He moved closer to his father. "You gave your word to Allah. That means you must follow through."

Khalil, flanked by the Kings and Knights, glided toward the throne, but hesitated several moments before he claimed the seat. "I will serve as interim ruler until you are ready to take your place here, Kamran."

"I do not—"

"Kamran, you *will* take your place here," Khalil insisted, placing a firm hand on his shoulder. "There is no greater person to create reform here in Durabia, than a king with the heart, compassion, and the wisdom to lead the way." Khalil allowed his hands fall by his side. "But with your permission, I will clean house and implement a system where all of the Nationals are in line with becoming productive members of your kingdom. Trust me on that."

Epilogue

Ellena stared through the wall of glass, oblivious to her surroundings. She was beautiful and serene in a loose, white tunic that complemented her radiant skin.

Beyond the plate glass, the tranquil blue waters were hypnotic and flowed from the Jumillah Hotel, to the palace and beyond, then spread out and around central downtown.

Kamran settled on the love seat next to Ellena, hating the faraway look in her eyes. Her experience in Nadaum had damaged her soul. The very thing she feared had happened, and he'd been powerless to protect her.

The entire horrific incident made Kamran understand that unless he moved Durabia in a direction where women and people of all ethnic backgrounds were accepted, the country would not transform to a place where his own wife had nothing to fear. And it would not be a place that his children had nothing to fear.

Kamran stroked the back of his hand down the side of her face and watched as her mouth bloomed into a wide smile. "Are you okay, my love?"

Ellena gazed into his eyes and said, "I am perfectly all right."

He leaned in and ran his tongue across her lips before capturing them in a passionate kiss. He ended their sensuous interlude, saying, "And it is my job to keep you that way."

And he meant it. Kamran would focus his energy on grooming his nephew Hassan, and also calling forth other members of the Maharaj family who had left Durabia because of its harsh laws and standing on various matters. He planned to make things right. But first, he would help restore his beloved's equilibrium. For days, she would not let their children out of her sight. Even Saba, and the nannies had to keep them in whatever room Ellena happened to be in at the moment.

Since her return, Ellena had taken to sleeping in the open courtyard of the palace, surrounded by guards, with sheer curtains the only barrier between her and the outside world.

Kamran joined her there every night. No way would he spend those moments away from his beloved if it could be helped. Only this week, had she slowly made her way back to being in their bedroom or any enclosed place. He did not second guess her fears, he only knew they existed and despaired that she would ever be able to put them in the shadows, where they belonged.

Her reaction filled Kamran with sadness and made him reflect on his life here, his family's actions, his father's politics, and their place in the world. He had caught no end of backlash because a Black woman now sat on the throne of a Middle Eastern country—unheard of in this day and time and for centuries before now. Despite everything, he would not change this for the world. Ellena was the woman who had his heart and the one he needed by his side.

He folded her hand in his and squeezed to get her attention. When she shifted toward him, he gave her a half-smile. "You know how I have always said you are a gift to me that I would not return unopened?"

She dipped her head in acknowledgement, but focused on the river. "I remember."

"Well, you are more to me than that."

A beautiful smile lit her face. "Yes, my love. You know I feel the same way about you."

Now, he realized her value was immeasurable. Those moments where she defied his father came to mind more often these days. She expressed so much wisdom that he could find guidance in shifting Durabia in the right direction—a direction where people didn't squander their wealth or talents. A direction where women did not have to fear or tamp down on their gifts to make men feel good about themselves. Those daily discussions with Khalil highlighted many positives, as well.

The Kings of the Castle had been a bond of brotherhood that Kamran never realized would be the very thing to help chart how Durabia would advance in the future. All of his American brothers, from various ethnic backgrounds and religions, were working together for the good of the communities where they were raised in America, and now here in Durabia. They were a prime example of unity, integrity, and determination. Thoughts of establishing provinces to allow the same process to uplift local communities, meant Durabians, the Kings, Knights, Queens, and Ellena's family would play a major part in making this the metropolis Ellena had mentioned last year. And since Durabia was not a military focused country, he had already contracted with Calvin Atwood to develop a defense system to protect Durabia from its new enemies.

As much as he had insisted on Khalil remaining at the helm, the older man continuously brought Kamran in for consults on major decisions. More frequently, of late, he also hinted that it was time for Kamran to take his rightful place on the throne. Kamran was in no hurry. He couldn't be a great king until he was certain he was an even better husband. Ellena needed him more than anyone else did right now. The children did not seem as affected, but only time would show the truth.

Another thing he believed would make Ellena happy was figuring out a way to navigate her sister's legal troubles and bring her to Durabian soil. Unpacking that whole process for Amanda McCoy would take some time, and he might even have to do something not quite legal to extract her from the clutches of that Mississippi justice system. Thankfully, Christian and Blair were further along in their plans to come. Having more family around her would give Ellena a sense of peace. At least, he hoped that would be the case.

"Beloved," he said, trying to snatch her from her thoughts. "You need me to take over the little ones for a while?"

Ellena chuckled and answered, "So you're going to do a little babysitting?"

"Yes, to give you a break, knowing that I'm here." He brought her hand to his mouth and kissed her palm. "I worry about what those men did to you and the way they have held your mind hostage."

She gripped his hand and returned the gesture. "All this, because they wanted the throne. No one should have that much power over another."

"Sadly, it exists," he countered. "The issue is the person wielding that power. If they aren't coming from a righteous or spiritual place, then that power can be misused and corrupted. I want to put things in place that will probably make the neighboring countries a little upset."

"You mean, more upset than the possibility of me being on the throne?"

"That's not a possibility," he countered. "It is an absolute certainty."

Ellena averted her gaze to their conjoined hands. "Are you sure you want to be at odds with all of those countries Durabia has been aligned with all of these years? I don't need to be queen. I just want to be your wife."

"The two are mutually inclusive. You are my wife and my beloved. I just so happen to be the ruling Sheikh of Durabia, and by default, that makes you Sheikh. And that is that." He nodded as though that was the end of the conversation.

"And you think that I, being in this position, can contribute in some significant way?"

"My love, we cannot effect change, unless we, in any capacity, are able to shift the dynamics of how women and people of color, are viewed in my country. That is the change I would like to see here." He inhaled deeply, focused on the dreams for his kingdom. "All this time, in my visions it was always about making this the wealthiest place in the world. It was about economy and finance. The true wealth is establishing a place where people are accepted and appreciated for who they are and what they contribute. Everyone will play a vital part here. It is time that Durabia reflects that. It starts with you and me."

She embraced him and the sigh that escaped her lips was filled with weariness.

He held her closer to absorb it into himself. Seconds later, he kissed her forehead, then whispered, "I wish there was something I could do to take away your sadness."

"I think you misunderstand," she protested. "I'm not sad because of what happened to me."

Kamran flinched and his gaze bored into hers. "Then what?" He shook his head. "No, I do not understand."

After a heartfelt sigh, Ellena said, "I took the lives of all those men."

"In self-defense," he protested.

Shaking her head, she said, "True, but they didn't hurt me."

Kamran tilted her chin so he could look directly into her eyes. "They would have kept you bound and imprisoned if you had not participated in your own rescue."

"I should have known help was coming." With a hand to his jaw, she added, "That you would send them for me."

"If I didn't have so many guns pointed at my head, then I would have been on one of Daron's contraptions, riding in to save the day."

She gave him a smile that warmed his soul. "Knight in shining armor and all that."

"I do not know about this knight thing," he said with a shrug. "But I think King has a better ring to it."

Silence fell between them, then in a thoughtful tone, Kamran said, "Every day that I visit my family in that far off part of the palace—watching them flounder and find their way, at the mercy of everyone else's kindness—you don't know how close I've come to just ending it all."

Ellena gasped and leaned away from him. "You don't mean … killing them?"

He gave her a long, hard look. Yes, he meant exactly that. Their punishment was much too light.

"You should talk to me about these things," she said, laying her head against his broad chest. "Not let them fester and take up space in your heart."

Kamran pressed a kiss to her forehead. "I do not need you to be responsible for managing my anger. Not when I need to be fully present in your pain."

"No, my love," she whispered, cupping his face in her hands. "You cannot surrender to the darkness. That is their playground. We are not those people."

"What they did to you and my children was unthinkable," he said through his teeth.

In that moment, he identified the obstacle that kept him from accepting the full mantle of rulership. His anger was an entity unto itself—and he could not be fair-minded if he couldn't release it. What Ellena said made sense. Healing and forgiveness would take time, but with her help, he'd achieve both.

"That is true," she said in a low tone. "They let the darkness rule them. And if I am going to be queen, then the first command is that I will hold space for you in your anger and you will hold the same for my pain. We will get through this together."

Kamran wiped the tears streaming down her face as he held her, never wanting to let her go. Gently, he stroked her hair and after several minutes went by, sensed that her mood had shifted. He pulled away to meet her gaze. "You know, you never did tell me where you hid—"

"No, I didn't," she said, laughing as her eyes twinkled with mischief. "Did I?"

About the *Knights of the Castle* Series

Don't miss the hot new standalone series. The Kings of the Castle made them family, but the Knights will transform the world.

Book 1 - King of Durabia – Naleighna Kai

No good deed goes unpunished, or that's how Ellena Kiley feels after she rescues a child and the former Crown Prince of Durabia offers to marry her.

Kamran learns of a nefarious plot to undermine his position with the Sheikh and jeopardize his ascent to the throne. He's unsure how Ellena, the fiery American seductress, fits into the plan but she's a secret weapon he's unwilling to relinquish.

Ellena is considered a sister by the Kings of the Castle and her connection to Kamran challenges her ideals, her freedoms, and her heart. Plus, loving him makes her a potential target for his enemies. When Ellena is kidnapped, Kamran is forced to bring in the Kings.

In the race against time to rescue his woman and defeat his enemies, the kingdom of Durabia will never be the same.

Book 2 - Knight of Bronzeville – Naleighna Kai and Stephanie M. Freeman

Chaz Maharaj thought he could maintain the lie of a perfect marriage for his adoring fans ... until he met Amanda.

The connection between them should have ended with that unconditional "hall pass" which led to one night of unbridled passion. But once would never satisfy his hunger for a woman who could never be his. When Amanda walked out of his life, it was supposed to be forever. Neither of them could have anticipated fate's plan.

Chaz wants to explore his feelings for Amanda, but Susan has other ideas. Prepared to fight for his budding romance and navigate a plot that's been laid to crush them, an unexpected twist threatens his love and her life.

When Amanda's past comes back to haunt them, Chaz enlists the Kings of the Castle to save his newfound love in a daring escape.

Book 3 - Knight of South Holland – Karen D. Bradley

He's a brilliant inventor, but he'll decimate anyone who threatens his woman.

When the Kings of the Castle recommend Calvin Atwood, strategic defense inventor, to create a security shield for the kingdom of Durabia, it's the opportunity of a lifetime. The only problem—it's a two-year assignment and he promised his fiancée they would step away from their dangerous lifestyle and start a family.

Security specialist, Mia Jakob, adores Calvin with all her heart, but his last assignment put both of their lives at risk. She understands how important this new role is to the man she loves, but the thought that he may be avoiding commitment does cross her mind.

Calvin was sure he'd made the best decision for his and Mia's future, until enemies of the state target his invention and his woman. Set on a collision course with hidden foes, this Knight will need the help of the Kings to save both his Queen and the Kingdom of Durabia.

Book 4 - Lady of Jeffrey Manor – J. S. Cole and Naleighna Kai

He's the kingdom's most eligible bachelor. She's a practical woman on temporary assignment.

When surgical nurse, Blair Swanson, departed the American Midwest for an assignment in the Kingdom of Durabia she had no intention of finding love.

As a member of the Royal Family, Crown Prince Hassan has a responsibility to the throne. A loveless, arranged marriage is his duty, but the courageous American nurse is his desire.

When a dark secret threatens everything Hassan holds dear, how will he fulfill his royal duty and save the lady who holds his heart?

Book 5 - Knight of Grand Crossing – Hiram Shogun Harris, Naleighna Kai, and Anita L. Roseboro

Rahm did time for a crime he didn't commit. Now that he's free, taking care of the three women who supported him on a hellish journey is his priority, but old enemies are waiting in the shadows.

Rahm Fosten's dream life as a Knight of the Castle includes Marilyn Spears, who quiets the injustice of his rough past, but in his absence a new foe has infiltrated his family.

Marilyn Spears waited for many years to have someone like Rahm in her life. Now that he's home, an unexpected twist threatens to rip him away again. As much as she loves him, she's not willing to go where this new drama may lead.

Meanwhile, Rahm's gift to his Aunt Alyssa brings her to Durabia, where she catches the attention of wealthy surgeon, Ahmad Maharaj. Her attendance at a private Bliss event puts her under his watchful eye, but also in the crosshairs of the worst kind of enemy. Definitely the wrong timing for the rest of the challenges Rahm is facing.

While Rahm and Marilyn navigate their romance, a deadly threat has him and the Kings of the Castle primed to keep Marilyn, Alyssa, and his family from falling prey to an adversary out for bloody revenge.

Book 6 - Knight of Paradise Island – J. L. Campbell

Someone is killing women and the villain's next target strikes too close to the Kingdom of Durabia.

Dorian "Ryan" Bostwick is a protector and he's one of the best in the business. When a King of the Castle assigns him to find his former lover, Aziza, he stumbles upon a deadly underworld operating close to the Durabian border.

Aziza Hampton had just rekindled her love affair with Ryan when a night out with friends ends in her kidnapping. Alone and scared, she must find a way to escape her captor and reunite with her lover.

In a race against time, Ryan and the Kings of the Castle follow ominous clues into the underbelly of a system designed to take advantage of the vulnerable. Failure isn't an option and Ryan will rain down hell on earth to save the woman of his heart.

Book 7 - Knight of Irondale – J. L Woodson, Naleighna Kai, and Martha Kennerson

Neesha Carpenter is on the run from a stalker ex-boyfriend, so why are the police hot on her trail?

Neesha escaped the madness of her previous relationship only to discover the Chicago Police have named her the prime suspect in her ex's shooting. With her life spinning out of control, she turns to the one man who's the biggest threat to her heart—Christian Vidal, her high school sweetheart.

Christian has always been smitten with Neesha's strength, intelligence and beauty. He offers her safe haven in the kingdom of Durabia and will do whatever it takes to keep her safe, even enlisting the help of the Kings of the Castle.

Neesha and Christian's rekindled flame burns hotter even as her stay in the country places the Royal Family at odds with the American government.

As mounting evidence points to Neesha's guilt, Christian must ask the hard question … is the woman he loves being framed or did she pull the trigger?

Book 8 - Knight of Birmingham – Lori Hays and MarZe Scott

Single mothers who are eligible for release, have totally disappeared from the Alabama justice system.

Women's advocate, Meghan Turner, has uncovered a disturbing pattern and she's desperate for help. Then her worse nightmare becomes a horrific reality when her friend goes missing under the same mysterious circumstances.

Rory Tannous has spent his life helping society's most vulnerable. When he learns of Meghan's dilemma, he takes it personal. Rory has his own tragic past and he'll utilize every connection, even the King of the Castle, to help this intriguing woman find her friend and the other women.

As Rory and Meghan work together, the attraction grows and so does the danger. The stakes are high and they will have to risk their love and lives to defeat a powerful adversary.

Book 9 - Knight of Penn Quarter – Terri Ann Johnson and Michele Sims

Following an undercover FBI sting operation that didn't go as planned, Agent Mateo Lopez is ready to put the government agency in his rearview mirror.

A confirmed workaholic, his career soared at the cost of his love life which had crashed and burned until mutual friends arranged a date with beautiful, sharp-witted, Rachel Jordan, a rising star at a children's social services agency.

Unlucky in love, Rachel has sworn off romantic relationships, but Mateo finds himself falling for her in more ways than one. When trouble brews in one of Rachel's cases, he does everything in his power to keep her safe—even if it means resorting to extreme measures.

Will the choices they make bring them closer together or cost them their lives?

About the Kings of the Castle Series

"Did you miss The Kings of the Castle? "They are so expertly crafted and flow so well between each of the books, it's hard to tell each is crafted by a different author. Very well done!" - Lori H…, Amazon and Goodreads

Each King book 2-9 is a standalone, NO cliffhangers

Book 1 – Kings of the Castle, the introduction to the series and story of King of Wilmette (Vikkas Germaine)

USA TODAY, New York Times, and National Bestselling Authors work together to provide you with a world you'll never want to leave. The Castle.

Fate made them brothers, but protecting the Castle, each other, and the women they love, will make them Kings. Their combined efforts to find the current Castle members responsible for the attempt on their mentor's life, is the beginning of dangerous challenges that will alter the path of their lives forever.

These powerful men, unexpectedly brought together by their pasts and current circumstances, will become a force to be reckoned with.

King of Chatham - Book 2 – London St. Charles

While Mariano "Reno" DeLuca uses his skills and resources to create safe havens for battered women, a surge in criminal activity within the Chatham area threatens the women's anonymity and security. When Zuri, an exotic Tanzanian Princess, arrives seeking refuge from an arranged marriage and its deadly consequences, Reno is now forced to relocate the women in the shelter, fend off unforeseen enemies of The Castle, and endeavor not to lose his heart to the mysterious woman.

King of Evanston - Book 3 - J. L. Campbell

Raised as an immigrant, he knows the heartache of family separation firsthand. His personal goals and business ethics collide when a vulnerable woman stands to lose her baby in an underhanded and profitable scheme crafted by powerful, ruthless businessmen and politicians who have nefarious ties to The Castle. Shaz and the Kings of the Castle collaborate to uproot the dark forces intent on changing the balance of power within The Castle and destroying their mentor.

National Bestselling Author, J.L. Campbell presents book 3 in the Kings of the Castle Series, featuring Shaz Bostwick.

King of Devon - Book 4 - Naleighna Kai

When a coma patient becomes pregnant, Jaidev Maharaj's medical facility comes under a government microscope and media scrutiny. In the midst of the investigation, he receives a mysterious call from someone in his past that demands that more of him than he's ever been willing to give and is made aware of a dark family secret that will destroy the people he loves most.

King of Morgan Park - Book 5 - Karen D. Bradley

Two things threaten to destroy several areas of Daron Kincaid's life—the tracking device he developed to locate victims of sex trafficking and an inherited membership in a mysterious outfit called The Castle. The new developments set the stage to dismantle the relationship with a woman who's been trained to make men weak or put them on the other side of the grave. The secrets Daron keeps from Cameron and his inner circle only complicates an already tumultuous situation caused by an FBI sting that brought down his former enemies. Can Daron take on his enemies, manage his secrets and loyalty to the Castle without permanently losing the woman he loves?

King of South Shore - Book 6 - MarZe Scott

Award-winning real estate developer, Kaleb Valentine, is known for turning failing communities into thriving havens in the Metro Detroit area. His plans to rebuild his hometown neighborhood are dereailed with one phone call that puts Kaleb deep in the middle of an intense criminal investigation led by a detective who has a personal vendetta. Now he will have to deal with the ghosts of his past before they kill him.

King of Lincoln Park - Book 7 – Martha Kennerson

Grant Khambrel is a sexy, successful architect with big plans to expand his Texas Company. Unfortunately, a dark secret from his past could destroy it all unless he's willing to betray the man responsible for that success, and the woman who becomes the key to his salvation.

King of Hyde Park - Book 8 -Lisa Dodson

Alejandro "Dro" Reyes has been a "fixer" for as long as he could remember, which makes owning a crisis management company focused on repairing professional reputations the perfect fit. The same could be said of Lola Samuels, who is only vaguely aware of his "true" talents and seems to be oblivious to the growing attraction between them. His company, Vantage Point, is in high demand and business in the Windy City is booming. Until a mysterious call following an attempt on his mentor's life forces him to drop everything and accept a fated position with The Castle. But there's a hidden agenda and unexpected enemy that Alejandro doesn't see coming who threatens his life, his woman, and his throne.

King of Lawndale - Book 9 - Janice M. Allen

Dwayne Harper's passion is giving disadvantaged boys the tools to transform themselves into successful men. Unfortunately, the minute he steps up to take his place among the men he considers brothers, two things stand in his way: a political office that does not want the competition Dwayne's new education system will bring, and a well-connected former member of The Castle who will use everything in his power—even those who Dwayne mentors—to shut him down.

Naleighna Kai is the *USA TODAY, Essence®*, and national bestselling and award-winning author of several women's fiction, contemporary fiction, Christian fiction, Romance, erotica, and science fiction novels that plumb the depth of unique relationships and women's issues. She is also a contributor to a New York Times bestseller, one of AALBC's 100 Top Authors, a member of CVS Hall of Fame, Mercedes Benz Mentor Award Nominee, and the E. Lynn Harris Author of Distinction.

In addition to successfully cracking the code of landing a deal for herself and others with a major publishing house, she continues to "pay it forward" by organizing the annual Cavalcade of Authors which gives readers intimate access to the most accomplished writing talent today. She also serves as CEO of Macro Marketing & Promotions Group which offers aspiring and established authors assistance with ghostwriting, developmental editing, publishing, marketing, and other services to jump-start or enhance their writing careers. She also founded NK Tribe Called Success for her clients who participate in literary events and media advertising as a group and produce creative projects and anthologies.

CPSIA information can be obtained
at www.ICGtesting.com
Printed in the USA
JSHW030200050623
42679JS00005B/256